The Secret
of the
Ghostly Hot Rod

Bethany House Books by
Bill Myers

Bloodhounds, Inc.
CHILDREN'S MYSTERY SERIES

The Ghost of KRZY
The Mystery of the Invisible Knight
Phantom of the Haunted Church
Invasion of the UFOs
Fangs for the Memories
The Case of the Missing Minds
The Secret of the Ghostly Hot Rod

Nonfiction

The Dark Side of the Supernatural
Hot Topics, Tough Questions

Bill Myers' Web site: www.BillMyers.com

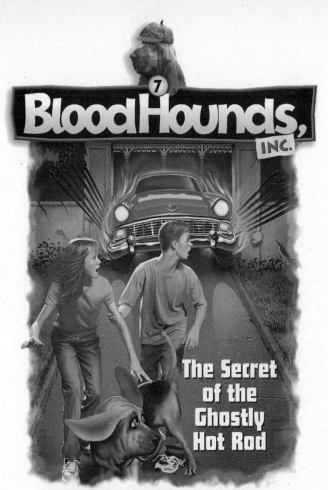

7
BloodHounds,
INC.

The Secret
of the
Ghostly
Hot Rod

Bill Myers

with David Wimbish

BETHANY HOUSE PUBLISHERS
MINNEAPOLIS, MINNESOTA 55438

The Secret of the Ghostly Hot Rod
Copyright © 2000
Bill Myers

Cover illustration by William Graf
Cover design by Lookout Design Group, Inc.

Published by Bethany House Publishers
A Ministry of Bethany Fellowship International
11400 Hampshire Avenue South
Minneapolis, Minnesota 55438
www.bethanyhouse.com

Printed in the United States of America by
Bethany Press International, Minneapolis, Minnesota 55438

Library of Congress Cataloging-in-Publication Data

CIP data applied for

ISBN 1–55661–491–8   CIP

For Robin Jones Gunn . . .

a friend and writer
also committed to reaching our youth.

Contents

1. The Case Begins 9
2. "He's Come Back for Me!" 20
3. From Booze to Boos! 33
4. Winkin', Blinkin', and . . . Jeremiah? 42
5. Now, That's Speed Skating! 55
6. Roadkill on the Highway of Life 67
7. Elvis, Is That You? 78
8. Burnin' Rubber! 91
9. Sneeze the Day 103
10. Rocket Girl 111

". . . Do not turn to mediums
or seek out spiritists,
for you will be defiled by them."

Leviticus 19:31, NIV

1

The Case Begins

MONDAY, 12:25 PDST

Fifty thousand people were on their feet, screaming their lungs out. It was the bottom of the ninth. Two outs. Center City, four, Midvale, three. Midvale was down to its last out in the biggest baseball game of the new century. And Sean Hunter strode confidently to the plate, carrying his famous bat, "Big Bertha," the source of so many thrills for Midvale fans throughout the years.

The cheers grew even louder as "Homerun" Hunter stepped into the batter's box, wiggling his bat back and forth.

The Center City pitcher went into his windup.

The noise from the crowd was deafening.

Whoosh! Sean let the first ball go by.

"Stee-rike one!" the umpire cried.

Sean could hear the loud thumping of his heart over the roar of the crowd.

Here came pitch number two.

This time he swung the bat with all of his might!

Swoosh!

And missed.

"Stee-rike twooooooooo!"

He backed out of the batter's box, took a deep breath, and let it out. It was now or never.

The pitcher stared in to get the sign from his catcher.

Sean stared back just as hard. He wanted to be sure he saw the ball the moment the pitcher let it fly.

The pitcher went into his windup.

Here it came.

Sean swung so hard he almost came out of his shoes. And this time . . .

K-POW!

. . . he connected!

He dropped his bat and sprinted for first as fast as he could. The ball sailed high and deep, toward the center-field fence. As he rounded first base, he saw the ball bounce off the top of the fence and ricochet away from the center fielder.

He passed second base and headed for third, glancing

over his shoulder to see the outfielder still chasing the ball.

In the stands, the Midvale fans were going crazy. "Run, Sean, run!"

By the time he reached third, the outfielder had retrieved the ball and was firing it toward home plate.

"Stop!" shouted the third-base coach. "Stop!"

"Stop!" screamed the fifty thousand people in the stands. "Stop!"

But Sean wasn't stopping. If he could make it home, the game would be tied, and then Midvale might have a chance to win it in extra innings. On the other hand, if the game ended with him stuck on third base . . .

He pushed the thought out of his mind. Home plate lay just ahead. He saw the catcher's eyes watching the ball sailing toward him.

This was going to be close!

Suddenly Sean's legs began sticking to the ground.

He looked down.

Quicksand?!

Who in the world had put quicksand down the third-base line?

It grew deeper and deeper until it was all Sean could do just to keep moving!

And then he saw it. An alligator. *An alligator?!* The

11

huge beast lay on the base path in front of him, hissing and snapping its giant jaws.

What's going on? Sean thought. *Surely it must be against the rules to have an alligator on the playing field.* He made a mental note to check the rule book as soon as the game ended.

Meanwhile, the alligator nipped at Sean and missed . . . barely. Once again the big reptile's mouth opened and snapped shut. This time Sean jumped in the air and landed on its nose . . . then he ran all the way down its back and leaped off its tail.

Now all he had to do to score the tying run was get around Mrs. Tubbs. *Mrs. Tubbs?!* And her fat cat, Precious. *Precious?!* (Is there an echo around here?) What on earth were Mrs. Tubbs and Precious doing on the field? And why were they playing for Center City? This was crazy! Everyone knew Mrs. Tubbs lived in Midvale!

"HISSS! YEOWWRR!" Precious extended his paws and swiped viciously at Sean's leg.

"You brat!" Mrs. Tubbs yelled at Sean. "Just look what you did to my geraniums!"

Once again, Sean looked down. Sure enough, he was standing right on top of Mrs. Tubbs' prize geraniums.

He did a quick side step and moved neatly around them and Mrs. Tubbs.

In front of him, the Center City catcher had already caught the ball and was bracing for the collision.

Sean knew he'd have to try to jar the ball loose.

Suddenly the catcher ripped off his mask to make the tag. Wait a minute! Make that *her* mask. *Her mask?!* (There's that echo again.)

It was Melissa!

What was his sister doing playing catcher for the Center City Cyclones?

"Sean!" she shouted. "Sean, wake up!"

Sean moaned and opened his eyes. Where was he?

"Sean, wake up! You're supposed to be paying attention!"

He blinked the sleep out of his eyes as he looked up into the angry face of his sister. She stood over him, her arms folded across her chest.

He sat up groggily and looked around. Off to his left, marble cherubs surrounded an ornate birdbath, all of them gracefully spitting water into the air.

To his right, a small grove of peach trees stood against the blue summer sky.

Oh, that's right! he remembered. *The peach trees!*

"Sorry," he muttered, "I guess I must have fallen asleep."

"We're supposed to be keeping an eye on those trees," his sister scolded him.

"I know, I know." He yawned and struggled to his feet. "But come on . . . I mean, who's gonna be stealing peaches?"

Melissa's anger didn't soften. "I don't care. Mrs. Sanks hired us to keep an eye on her peaches . . . and for $250, the least *you* can do is stay awake!"

"I told her it was just a squirrel stealing them," he said defensively. "Besides, what's the big deal? She has enough money to buy all the peaches she wants." He made a big, sweeping gesture. "I mean, just look at this place!"

It was true. The widow Sanks's mansion was known as the biggest and best house in Midvale. Her property consisted of twenty acres here on the top of Snob Hill, where she lived surrounded by trees, flowers, fountains, and beautifully manicured lawns that would have been the envy of any golf course. If she wanted something to eat or drink, all she had to do was ring a bell and one of her servants brought it on a silver tray.

Yet she had offered Sean and Melissa's detective agency, Bloodhounds, Incorporated, $250 to find out who was stealing peaches from her small orchard.

Sean looked around. "By the way," he asked, "where's Slobs?"

"Oh, she's . . ."

"WOOF! WOOF!" came the answer as 102 pounds

14

of bloodhound bounded past, hot on the trail of a cottontail bunny. The rabbit disappeared into a patch of bushes that looked too thick for Slobs to enter.

But the dog charged right in, barking and yapping all the way.

"She loves it here, doesn't she?" Melissa laughed, her anger slowly melting away.

"Can you blame her?" Sean asked.

"Woof! Woof!"

The rabbit emerged from the bushes and ran so fast he was little more than a blur.

Slobs stayed right behind him.

Around the fountain they went. Once . . . twice . . . three times!

Then in and out among the peach trees. Slobs kicked up dust and dirt at every turn, but she still managed to stay right on the animal's tail.

What the poor bunny didn't know was that Slobs— for all her ferocious barking and snapping—was really a big marshmallow. She wouldn't hurt a fly . . . and if the rabbit had decided to stand his ground and fight, Slobs probably would have turned and run. She wasn't interested in hurting anyone. She just enjoyed the chase.

Finally, tired of running around in circles, the rabbit took off in a straight shot, with Slobs right behind.

"Sean!" Melissa yelled. "Stop her! She's headed for the street!"

"So?"

"So? Don't you remember the case of the invisible knight? How we almost lost her! What if she gets hit by a car again?"

"A car?" Sean scoffed. "What car?" He gestured toward the quiet, shady boulevard that ran past Mrs. Sanks's mansion. "There hasn't been a car on that street all—"

VAROOM! VAROOM!

Sean's words were drowned out by the roar of an automobile. It flew around the corner out of nowhere. Thick black smoke poured out behind it as it rocketed toward them.

It was bright red . . . with huge yellow and orange flames painted on the hood and down the side. It was a Chevy. Sean remembered that from the old movies. A classic 1956 Chevy. A 1956 classic Chevy that was heading straight for their beloved bloodhound!

"Slobs!" he yelled. "Get out of the street! Get out of the street!"

But Slobs didn't get out of the street. Instead, she stopped and stood still as the speeding car bore down upon her.

"Slobs!"
Too late!

SCREE . . .

The driver slammed on the brakes. The car swerved back and forth, leaving black skid marks all across the road.

. . . EEEE . . .

It was twenty feet away from Slobs and closing in fast.
Fifteen feet!

. . . EEEECH . . .

Ten!
Still, Slobs did not move.
Melissa sprinted into the street, determined to push the dog out of the way.
"Melissa! Don't!" Sean yelled.
Five feet!
Then, at the last possible second, Slobs jumped off to the side.
Melissa leaped out of the way, falling hard, just as the hot rod roared past her. Its tires smoked as it slid down the road. Finally, it came to a sideways stop twenty feet or so away.

Sean raced to his sister. "Misty! Misty, are you okay?!" He reached down and pulled her to her feet.

"No!" she yelled. "I'm not all right! I'm mad!"

She spun around and started running down the street toward the hot rod. "You could've killed somebody!" she shouted.

The car sat there with its engine idling and its doors closed.

"Are you crazy?" Melissa yelled. "You can't drive ninety miles an hour in a neighborhood like this!"

Still no response.

The hot rod's driver seemed content to sit quietly and hide behind his car's tinted windows . . . which only made Melissa madder.

Finally, she arrived at the car, and before Sean could stop her, she began banging on the driver's window.

"I want an apology!" she shouted.

Sean had never seen his sister so furious—except for the time he'd eaten the entire cake she'd baked as her final project for home economics class. (Actually, he felt she should have thanked him for saving her from failing. He wasn't sure what she'd put in it, but whatever it was, it sure did a number on his stomach. For the next three days, he'd been afraid to be more than twenty steps from the bathroom!)

As she banged on the car, he came up behind her and

put his hand on her shoulder. "Come on, sis, it's all right . . . nobody's hurt."

She pulled away from him and prepared for another round of window thumping. But before she landed the first blow, the driver's door suddenly swung open.

Sean and Melissa jumped back. Both gasped at the same time. And for good reason.

Nobody was driving! The driver's seat was completely empty!

Suddenly the widow Sanks hobbled out her front door. "That's him!" she shouted. "That's my son! He's come back from the dead!"

At the sound of her voice, the car door slammed shut.

SCREECH . . .

The tires burned rubber as the hot rod shot off down the street.

Sean, Melissa, and Slobs stood watching as it rounded the bend in the road and disappeared. And then, at that exact moment, the engine noise stopped. Completely.

It was as if the car had completely vanished.

2

"He's Come Back for Me!"

MONDAY, 12:55 PDST

"Did you see him?" Mrs. Sanks screamed. "Did you see my son?"

"Mrs. Sanks." Melissa swallowed hard and continued. "I got a good look and . . . and . . ."

"And what?"

Sean finished his sister's sentence. "And nobody was driving the car!"

"Of course somebody was driving," the widow cried. "It was my son . . . come back from the dead."

The frail old woman eased herself down on the curb. Then she buried her face in her hands and began to cry.

Sean and Melissa exchanged worried looks. They didn't know what to think. What was all this "My son's come back from the dead" stuff?

20

"Oh, Willy," the widow sobbed. "Are you still angry with me? After all these years, are you still mad? If only you knew how much I love you!"

Melissa kneeled down and sat next to the sobbing woman. "Are you okay, Mrs. Sanks?" she asked.

The widow nodded.

SKRONKKK!

Startled by the sound, Sean jumped about eighteen inches into the air. He thought the mysterious hot rod was coming back, honking its horn, until he saw it was only Mrs. Sanks, blowing her nose.

"I should have told you right from the start," Mrs. Sanks sniffed.

"Told us what?" Melissa asked. She scooted closer to the old woman and put her arm around her to comfort her. She didn't notice the few strands of the widow's hair that caught in the band of her wristwatch.

"I didn't really hire you to watch my peach trees," the woman said. Then she sobbed violently, once again lowering her head into her hands.

What Sean saw made him blink in surprise. When Mrs. Sanks put her head down, her hair didn't go with her. Instead, it seemed to be floating in the air! Man, oh man! He'd seen enough weird things for one day.

Then it hit him. The hair wasn't floating. It was

21

dangling from Melissa's wrist. Mrs. Sanks wore a wig!

And Melissa didn't even notice. "Well, then . . . why *did* you hire us?" she was asking.

Sean pointed and stammered, trying to get his sister's attention. "Ummm . . . mmmm . . . hmmm . . ."

She shot him a dirty look until she turned to see what he was pointing at. Then she gasped in spite of herself. "Oh my!"

Fortunately, Mrs. Sanks didn't notice as she continued her story. "I hired you because I wanted you to find out why my son has come back with that car of his!"

"Your *dead* son?" Sean asked.

"That's right," the woman nodded. "Say, is it just me, or is it getting cold all of a sudden?"

Trying not to be noticed, Melissa yanked hard on the wig, trying to free it from her watchband. But it was just too tangled.

"Mrs. Sanks," Sean said, "I'm sorry, but we really don't believe in ghosts and things like that."

Melissa yanked at the wig again and again until she finally managed to free it.

Ker-plop!

It landed on Mrs. Sanks's head sideways, making her look like that guy from The Three Stooges.

Melissa tried to straighten it, but Sean shook his

head. In this situation, it was better to leave well enough alone.

Mrs. Sanks sighed. "I didn't believe in ghosts, either, until . . ." Her voice trailed off.

"Until what?" Melissa prompted her.

"Until last Thursday night. That's when my Willy came back. Driving that old car of his. The car he was killed in."

"Killed in?" Sean asked. He could feel the hair on the back of his neck starting to stand up.

Mrs. Sanks dabbed at her eyes with the sleeve of her sweater. "He was only seventeen . . . a good boy . . . but he was going through a rebellious stage. Drinking . . . and driving too fast. My, how he loved that old car."

"Go on, Mrs. Sanks," Melissa encouraged.

"He'd been drinking, and I told him I wasn't going to put up with it anymore. He ran out of the house and drove off in that car of his. That was the last time I saw him alive."

"What happened?" Sean asked.

"They said he was traveling over one hundred miles an hour when he went off the Old Mountain Road." She swallowed hard. "The car blew up. They told me he died instantly."

Sean and Melissa sat in silence for a long moment, not knowing what to say. Finally Melissa spoke. "I'm sorry, Mrs. Sanks, that's so sad."

"But why do you think . . . ?" Sean hesitated.

"Why has he come back?" Mrs. Sanks asked. "I don't know. That's why I hired you—to help me find out what he wants." With great effort she rose to stand up. Melissa took her arm and helped. "I'm an old woman," she said. "I don't have much time left. Maybe he's come back for me. Maybe . . ."

"Maybe what?" asked Sean.

"Maybe he just wants me to know he forgives me . . . and that he loves me."

Before the kids could respond, they heard another woman's voice behind them. "Mrs. Sanks, what are you doing out here?"

They turned to the sweetly smiling face of Gretchen, Mrs. Sanks's personal nurse. She was dressed in her dazzling white uniform, which, as usual, was starched to military perfection. Gretchen was in her thirties, tall, thin, very pretty, and totally dedicated to her employer.

"It's too cold for you to be out here like this," she gently chided. "And you can't afford to get too excited." She tapped herself on the chest. "Your heart, you know."

Mrs. Sanks nodded. "I know . . . I know."

She took Gretchen's arm, and the two of them slowly began making their way back toward the house.

Just before they reached the porch, Mrs. Sanks turned

around and called over her shoulder, "If you help me find out what he wants, I'll pay you another $250!" With that, she headed up the porch and disappeared inside.

"Did you hear that?" Sean said to his sister. "That makes $500! Just think what we could do with all that money!"

"I don't know, Sean. It just seems so . . . weird."

"She's right! Weird!" someone said in a strange electronic-sounding voice. "And dangerous! Leave it alone! Remember . . . a coward dyes a thousand shirts . . . but a brave man is likely to get his clock cleaned."

The voice came from Sean's wrist. A green-faced leprechaun-like figure was staring up from Sean's watch, his eyes wide with fright.

"Hi, Jeremiah," Sean said. "I think the saying goes, 'A coward dies a thousand deaths, but a brave man only one.' "

"Whatever!" the little fellow shrugged. "I just think we ought to go on home and forget all about this. We've chased phantoms . . . flying saucers . . . we've tangled with vampires . . . and done lots of other strange stuff. But I won't do ghosts. No, sir!"

Jeremiah—which stood for *Johnson Electronic Reductive Entity Memory Inductive Assembly Housing*—was the creation of the kids' scientist friend, Doc. Jeremiah was a nervous bundle of electrical energy who seemed to get all of his important ideas from bumper stickers and fortune cookies. The only problem was that he tended to get everything all twisted up, so you could never be quite sure what he was talking about.

Sean, Melissa, and Doc were the only three who knew about Jeremiah, and they were determined to keep it that way . . . for everyone's sake. You never knew where Jeremiah might show up—on video games, a television set, Sean's watch . . . or anywhere else there was a monitor. Sometimes, when electronic conditions were just right, he was even able to become part of the real world.

"Jeremiah," Sean scolded, "you know there's no such thing as a ghost!"

"Of course not!" Jeremiah said, with more than a touch of sarcasm. "And there's no such thing as little electric men who live inside digital watches, either. But here I am. And I'm telling you, *something* was driving that car!"

"But think about it," Sean protested. "Five hundred dollars!"

"All the money in the world isn't going to help you when that ghost is sucking the blood out of you!" Jeremiah responded.

"Vampires suck blood, Jeremiah, not ghosts," Melissa corrected.

"Well . . . who knows what ghosts do? I, for one,

don't plan to stick around and find out!" There was a small popping noise, followed by a tiny flash . . . and the little guy disappeared to whatever TV or computer monitor he chose.

Melissa rolled her eyes. "I'm glad he's gone," she said.

"Me too," Sean agreed. "For such a feisty little guy, he can be a big coward sometimes. Speaking of big, where's Slobs?"

Melissa glanced around. "Over there!"

The big dog was in the middle of the street, her nose to the ground, sniffing furiously at something.

The two walked over to get a better look.

"What is it, girl?" Melissa asked. "What do you smell?"

Slobs didn't look up. She kept right on sniffing with her nose about a half inch from the street.

Sean bent over and touched the asphalt with his finger. "It's oil," he said. "Looks like our ghost car was leaking oil."

"Maybe she can follow the trail," said Melissa, cringing as her brother wiped his oily finger on his pants.

"That's just what I was thinking," Sean agreed. He knelt down and whispered into Slobs' ear. "Go get it, girl. Take us to the ghost car!"

"WOOF! WOOF!"

For fifteen minutes, the young detectives followed Slobs, who was completely caught up by the mysterious trail she followed. A squirrel skittered in front of her, and she didn't even notice. A rabbit bounded across her path, and she didn't even care.

That's how it is with bloodhounds. Once they start tracking a scent, just about nothing will take their minds off it.

"This'll be great," Sean said. "She'll take us right to the car . . . we'll prove there's no ghost involved, and we'll pick up our $500! This is going to be the easiest money we've ever made!"

Slobs still had her nose to the ground as they followed her around the bend in the street. Then suddenly she stopped.

She lifted her head, sniffed the air, and whined.

"What is it, girl?" Sean asked. "What's wrong?"

Slobs began running back and forth across the street, sniffing and whining like a puppy who couldn't find her mother.

"She's lost the scent," Melissa said.

Slobs whined again, snorted in disgust, then suddenly lay down in the middle of the road, defeated.

Melissa was right. She had lost the trail. One minute it was there, the next it was gone. It was as if the old hot rod *really had* vanished into thin air.

"Well, that's just great," Sean grumbled. "What do we do now?"

Melissa shrugged. "I don't know. This one's got me nervous. Maybe we'd better go talk to the police."

MONDAY, 14:05 PDST

At the Midvale Police Department, Sean and Melissa were surprised to find Chief of Police John Robertson filling in for the desk sergeant. He was looking down, doing paper work. He was so engrossed that he hadn't even noticed them walk in.

"Ahem," Sean cleared his throat.

No response.

"AHEM!"

Startled, the chief looked up. "Oh . . . hi, guys. How are things over at Hound Dogs, Incorporated?"

"That's Bloodhounds," Melissa corrected him.

"Oh yeah, Bloodhounds," the chief grinned. He seemed embarrassed, as if the kids had caught him doing something wrong. He quickly shuffled his papers, trying to hide something—but he wasn't fast enough for Melissa. She'd seen that he wasn't doing paper work at all. He'd been playing a handheld video game.

She giggled. "Slow day, Chief?"

"We've had a few of 'em lately," he said, slipping the game into the nearest drawer, acting as if nothing were wrong. "And if you ask me, it's about time."

Suddenly a nervous smile spread across his face. "I don't suppose you two dropped by just to say hello, did you?"

"No, we didn't," Sean answered.

Chief Robertson sighed. "That's what I was afraid of. What is it this time? Zombies? Space monsters? Giant lizards?"

"No," Melissa said. "A car."

"A car? Is that all?" The chief let out a sigh of relief. "So . . ." he said, pushing himself back in his chair, "what happened? Somebody speeding? Run a red light? Forget to fasten his seat belt?"

"Nothing like that," Melissa answered.

"What, then?"

"We sort of had a run-in with a ghost car," Sean explained.

"A ghost car." The chief chuckled and shook his head. "I should have known with you two. What did this 'ghost car' do?"

"It came flying around the corner about ninety miles an hour—" Sean began.

"And almost ran over Slobs," Melissa interrupted.

"Slobs?" the chief asked. "Is that the kid who likes to eat all the time?"

"No, that's Bear," Sean said. "You know . . . Slobs." He pointed to their big dog, who sat quietly by the door, doing her two favorite things . . . sleeping and drooling.

The chief peered over the top of his desk. "Oh, *that* Slobs. My goodness . . . looks like we're going to need a mop." He turned back to the kids. "So what makes you so sure this was a ghost car?"

"Well," said Melissa, "for one thing, nobody was driving!"

"Maybe you just couldn't see the driver—"

"Oh, I could see, all right," Melissa interrupted. "The door flew open and there was nobody inside."

"That's right," Sean agreed. "Then the door slammed shut and the car took off. But as soon as it went around the corner . . . *poof*!"

"*Poof?*" Chief Robertson asked.

"*Poof*," Melissa repeated. "It just kind of disappeared."

The chief shook his head. "If anybody else told me something like that, I'd say he was crazy."

"We're not crazy, Chief," Sean said.

"Oh, believe me, after all we've been through with

you two, I know that. But tell me, what did this ghost car look like?"

Sean thought for a moment. "I think it was a '56 Chevy like you see in the movies. It was bright red . . . and it had big flames painted on the hood and down the sides."

Suddenly the color drained from the chief's face. He swallowed hard. "Did it have a big pair of fuzzy dice hanging from the rearview mirror?" he asked.

"Yeah, now that you mention it, it did!" Melissa exclaimed. "You know this car?"

The chief's hands had begun to shake. "It's . . . it's . . . no, that's impossible. It can't be."

"What, Chief?" Sean asked.

"It sounds like W-Willy Sanks," he stuttered. His voice grew louder and more frightened. "He swore he'd get even with me. Maybe . . . maybe he really did come back from the dead!"

3

From Booze to Boos!

MONDAY, 14:20 PDST

Chief Robertson called one of the other officers to take his place at the front desk. He then took Sean, Melissa, and Slobs back to his office so they could talk in private. Normally, the chief wasn't afraid of anyone or anything, but he was still shaking as he rummaged through his desk drawer.

"I know I have a bottle of aspirin in here somewhere," he mumbled. "Ah, here it is." He tried to open the bottle, but his hands were shaking so badly he couldn't do it.

"I . . . I'm sorry," he stammered, looking to Sean, "but . . . d-do you think you could help me?"

"Here, let me do that," Melissa offered. She took the bottle, snapped off the lid, and handed it back to the chief.

But when he tried to pour out a couple of aspirin, they flew everywhere—over his shoulder, onto the floor, into his shirt pocket. After a half dozen tries, he finally managed to get two of the little white tablets clutched tightly in his hand. He then popped them into his mouth. And with Melissa's help, he managed to raise a cup of cold water to his lips.

Trying to comfort the man, Sean said, "It's gonna be okay, Chief. First of all, we don't believe people can come back from the dead. But even if it was Willy Sanks, what's the worst he could do to you?"

Unfortunately, that made the chief suck in his breath just as the aspirin had started down his throat.

GAZORKSNFFFF!

The two tiny tablets shot out of his nose . . . at speeds in excess of a Randy Johnson fast ball.

Sean ducked as the little missiles whizzed past his head and . . .

PING!

. . . ricocheted off the wall and . . .

KA-ZING!

. . . shot upward into the ceiling fan and . . .

PING KA-ZING!

. . . bounced off the family photo the chief kept on his desk and finally landed . . .

YI-GULP!

. . . straight in the chief's gaping mouth, which had been their intended destination all along.

For a long moment the chief said nothing. When he finally did speak, all he said was "It was 1961. . . ."

"Pardon me?" Sean asked.

"That was when it happened." He sighed and continued. "Willy and I were co-captains on the Midvale High School basketball team. We had a great team that year. Came close to winning the state championship. . . ."

"And then?" Melissa asked gently.

"Willy Sanks started coming late to practice with booze on his breath. Then right before one of the biggest games of the year, he didn't come to practice at all. Claimed he had the flu. But on my way home that night, his hot rod flew past me, and someone threw a whiskey bottle out the driver's window."

"What did you do?" Sean asked.

"I didn't do anything," Chief replied. "But somebody else did. They knew what he was up to and turned him in. They searched his locker at school and found a pint of gin. Coach kicked him off the basketball team for good. I never did find out who snitched on him . . . but it wasn't me."

"Only he thought it was you," Melissa said.

"Oh yeah . . . he was really mad. Came by practice and threatened me. Told me he was going to get me if it was the last thing he ever did."

The chief shook his head a moment and continued. "Then he went out—driving around drunk—and got into a terrible accident and was killed. For weeks after that, I dreamed that Willy was coming back from the dead to get me. I'd wake up and think I saw him standing at the foot of my bed. It was awful! Just awful!"

"And now you really think he has come back from the dead," Sean asked.

Chief turned to him and quietly answered. "Wouldn't you?"

KA-THUNK!

The door to Chief Robertson's office flew open, and Melissa screamed. She spun around to see it was only the television reporter Rafael Ruelas. He was barging into the room, microphone in hand. Following him was a tall, thin man with a handheld camera, and a short, fat fellow who wore earphones while twisting dials on a contraption fastened to the utility belt around his waist.

"Chief," Ruelas said, "I hear there's a ghost in town

and there's a good chance he's looking for you!"

"What? Where did you . . . ?"

"Some people called the station," the reporter answered. "Said they saw something really weird out near the Sanks mansion. Seems this car was going about seventy miles an hour, when all of a sudden . . . *poof!* . . . it disappeared!"

"But . . . but what's that got to do with me?" the chief stuttered.

"I talked to Mrs. Sanks," Ruelas said. "She seems to think the ghost of her son is driving that car. And I've heard that you and Willy Sanks weren't exactly best friends during your days at Midvale High!"

He turned to his two assistants. "Are we rolling?"

The cameraman held up three fingers, then two, then one. "Rolling," he said.

Ruelas suddenly thrust his microphone in the chief's face.

"Tell me, Chief," he demanded. "Is it true that the city of Midvale is under attack from a ghost driving a souped-up '56 Chevy?"

"I don't want to talk about it," the chief responded. He pushed his chair away from his desk, got up, and strode out of his office.

But there was no getting away from Ruelas. He matched the chief stride for stride, keeping the microphone stuck in his face the whole time. The cameraman and sound man followed closely behind, their equipment beeping and whirring softly as they recorded every moment for Channel 42 News.

"Chief Robertson," Ruelas said loudly, "I'll ask you again! Is there any truth to the reports that a ghostly hot rod has been terrorizing the citizens of Midvale?"

They'd entered the booking room of the station, which grew deathly quiet. Conversations stopped in midsentence. Everyone seemed frozen, startled by the report of a phantom car loose in their city.

"No comment!" the chief responded.

"So you won't deny the story?" the reporter challenged.

"I have nothing more to say!"

With that, the chief turned on his heels and hurried out of the police station, leaving Melissa and Sean standing there with Ruelas and his crew.

Suddenly the reporter turned his attention to Melissa. "What about you? I understand you had an encounter with the demon car. Tell us what happened?"

"Well, we saw something," Melissa stammered. "But I don't believe it was a car driven by a ghost or anything like that."

"That's right," Sean chimed in. "I'm sure there's a

natural explanation for what we saw. We just have to find it."

Remembering the lessons from their last few cases, Melissa nodded. "We don't believe in ghosts," she said. "In fact, the Bible says that when someone dies, he's judged by God and goes to either heaven or hell. He doesn't hang around here as some sort of ghost."

"Whatever." Ruelas waved an impatient hand in Melissa's face. "But you still haven't told me what you saw!"

"A ghost!" an electronic voice chirped. "It was as plain as the toe on your face."

"What—who said that?" Ruelas demanded as his eyes shot around the room.

Sean clasped his hand over his wristwatch and whispered, "Jeremiah . . . shhh!"

"I did!" Jeremiah shouted. "I did!"

There was no use trying to shut him up. The little guy wasn't about to pass up the opportunity to become a TV star.

"Where are you?" Ruelas cried. He looked at his sound man, who shrugged.

"I'm right here!" Jeremiah shouted.

Sean was afraid something bad was about to happen, and he was right. All that running around the police department had stretched one of Ruelas's electrical cords beyond its limit, and it began to short out . . .

CRACKLE . . . CRACKLE . . . CRACKLE . . .

. . . until suddenly:

K-BOOM!

There was a flash of light and a tiny explosion. Suddenly a giant Jeremiah stood before them in all his green glory. All eight feet tall of green glory!

"What is he?" someone screamed.

"A monster!" another yelled.

"No!" someone shouted. "IT'S THE G-G-GHOST!"

Suddenly everyone stampeded for the doors. Everyone but the intrepid reporter Ruelas and his team. They stayed right there, with cameras and recorders rolling.

CRACKLE . . . CRACKLE . . . CRACKLE . . .
K-BOOOM!

Another flash! Another explosion! And Jeremiah was gone. He'd only been visible for a few seconds . . . but a few seconds was long enough.

Ruelas turned to his cameraman. "Did you get a shot of that . . . that ghost?"

The man patted his camera. "It's all right here."

"Great!" the reporter exclaimed. "We've got the story of a lifetime! Let's go!"

"No, wait!" Melissa shouted. "We can explain. That wasn't really a ghost. It was . . ."

Too late! The reporter and his crew were on their way back to the station with their precious videotape.

Jeremiah was about to become a TV star.

4

Winkin', Blinkin', and . . . Jeremiah?

MONDAY, 14:45 PDST

"Where do you suppose he went?" Melissa asked.

"Jeremiah?" Sean shrugged. "Who cares? It would be fine with me if he didn't show up anymore for a while."

"Yeah," Melissa agreed. "We gotta remember that whenever a room is full of electrical current, that sort of thing can happen. I just hope they didn't really get him on tape."

"We'll worry about that later," Sean said, rubbing his stomach. "Right now I'm too hungry to think about it."

"Didn't you put away three triple-decker cheeseburgers at lunch?"

"Yeah."

"And two large orders of fries?"

"Uh-huh." He glanced at his watch. "But that was nearly two hours ago."

Melissa shook her head. Her brother's appetite was amazing—a black hole from which no food could escape. And whenever the human eating-machine was hungry—which was often—he couldn't seem to think of anything else.

The two of them stood on the sidewalk at the intersection of Fourth and Main Streets. Slobs was busy doing her usual drooling routine beside them as they waited for the light to change.

Sean punched the Walk button again. "Man!" he grumbled. "What's taking so long? I wanna get home for dinner!"

Other people had also gathered on the corner, all of them waiting to cross the street. Melissa smiled at the pretty young mother pushing her baby in a stroller. Next to her, on a pair of crutches, was an athletic-looking man with a cast on his leg. And beside him was the old-timer everyone called Crazy Larry. He was pushing a shopping cart full of his "priceless treasures"—rusty cans, scraps of newspaper, and all sorts of odds and ends.

At last the light changed to green. Sean stepped out into the street, followed by Melissa, Slobs, and the others. But suddenly he stopped and groaned, "Oh no . . ."

"Oh no, what?" Melissa asked.

Sean pointed at the Walk signal.

A glowing greenish leprechaun was smiling out at them from inside the signal.

"Jeremiah!" Melissa whispered. "So that's where he went."

Jeremiah winked at them and was gone.

Immediately *Walk* changed to *Don't Walk*.

BEEP! BEEP!

A delivery truck had turned into the intersection, honking at them to get out of the way.

Sean, Melissa, and the others scampered back to the safety of the sidewalk. Everyone but Crazy Larry, who just stood in the middle of the street looking bewildered.

As soon as Sean and the others reached the curb, the signal—with Jeremiah once again inside it—flashed to *Walk*, and once again the small group bravely started back across Main Street.

HONK! HONK!

Oh no. Jeremiah had gone again, and *Don't Walk* was back.

Then *Walk*!

They started.

Then *Don't Walk*!

44

They stopped.
Walk!
They started.
Don't Walk!
Walk!
Don't Walk!
The group was running back and forth in the street as the signal changed faster and faster . . . and faster some more. But they weren't the only ones confused.

BEEP! BEEP!
HONK! HONK!

As traffic lights switched back and forth between green and red, drivers found it just as difficult to decide what to do.

SCREEECH!

Brakes squealed as a semi truck carrying bottles full of Olde Northe Maple Syrup charged into the intersection, only to be cut off by a pickup from Jackie's Chicken Farm.

KER-BLAM!

The big trucks slammed into each other.

K-RASH! K-RASH! K-RASH!

GLUG! GLUG! GLUG!

Jar after jar of maple syrup shattered as they hit the street, then began oozing a thick river of sticky brown liquid.

POCK! POCK! POCK
KA-POCK!

Feathers flew everywhere as the prize hens made their escape.

"LOOK OUT!"

SCREECH!
K-RASH!

Too late!

A dump truck full of manure couldn't stop in time and slammed into the truck from Jackie's Chicken Farm, spilling its entire cargo into the street.

EEEWWWW! Melissa held her nose. What a mess! A sticky, smelly, disgusting combination of maple syrup, chicken feathers, and fertilizer was everywhere!

And on everyone!

And still, the Jeremiah-infected traffic light kept flashing wildly back and forth between *Walk* and *Don't Walk* . . . from red to green and back again.

It was the worst traffic jam in Midvale history. Cars,

trucks, motorcycles, bicycles—all knotted together in an incredible mess of syrup, chicken feathers, and manure. And then suddenly:

KA-BLOOEY!

The Walk signal exploded in a flash of light, filling the air with thick white smoke.

"What do we do?" Melissa cried.

"Run!" Sean shouted.

Melissa couldn't have agreed more.

TUESDAY, 7:25 PDST

BRRRRT! BRRRRT!

Sean awoke the following morning to the chirping of his cell phone.

"Hello ... er ... I mean ... Bloodhounds, Incorporated ..."

BRRRRT! BRRRRT!

But it wasn't the phone he was holding in his hand. It was his shoe. "Where is that stupid phone?" he mumbled.

He sat up and poked around Slobs, who lay sprawled across the foot of the bed. She sighed, snorted, and went back to sleep.

BRRRRT! BRRRRT!

He pulled back the bedcovers. Nope, wasn't there, either.

BRRRRT! BRRRRT!

Where had he left it? Of course, it wasn't so easy finding it in all the mess. Sean prided himself on being a first-class, triple-A slob. Dresser drawers were half open with underwear, socks, and shirts hanging out. The floor was covered with books, CDs, videocassettes, clothes, and more. Much, much more.

BRRRRT! BRRRRT!

And somewhere in all of that mess, the cell phone continued to ring. Ah-hah! There it was! Underneath three pairs of dirty underwear.

BRRRR . . .

"Bloodhounds In—"
"Sean?" It was Spalding, the neighborhood rich kid.
"Hey, Spalding. What's up?"
"Apparently you and your sister are being featured on the news this morning," he said in his typically snooty tone.
"The news?"

"Channel 42. I believe it pertains to an automobile that is supposed to be haunting our area."

"Thanks!" Sean hung up and clicked on his TV.

"Sean?" Melissa knocked on his door.

"Come in," he called.

"Who was it?"

"Spalding. He says we're on the news." He motioned toward his bed. "Have a seat."

"Uh . . . that's okay," she said, looking around at the mess. "I think it'll be safer if I stand."

"Suit yourself."

Channel 42 was playing and replaying a tape of Jeremiah's appearance in the Midvale Police Station.

When she saw it, Melissa breathed a sigh of relief. The station's cameras had captured nothing more than a green blur. It was impossible to make out Jeremiah's features.

On the air, Rafael Ruelas was almost shouting into his microphone. "This amazing footage clearly shows the ghost that has been terrorizing the decent, law-abiding citizens of Midvale! A ghost with a thirst for speed and . . . apparently . . . revenge. There is some speculation that Midvale Chief of Police John Robertson is the object of the creature's anger."

Sean and Melissa exchanged looks.

Ruelas continued to rant. "After exhaustive research,

I was able to get an exclusive interview with two Midvale residents who were nearly run over by the ghost car."

Suddenly Melissa's face filled the TV screen:

"Well, we saw a car driven by a ghost," she heard herself say on the TV.

"I didn't say that!" Melissa shouted at the TV screen.

The camera pulled out to show Sean standing next to his sister. "That's right," he was saying. "There's not a natural explanation for what we saw."

"I didn't say that, either!" Sean shouted. "They've edited us! They've changed everything we said!"

Melissa moaned as she continued watching and hearing herself talk. "The Bible says that when someone dies, he hangs around here as some sort of ghost."

"How dare they change our words?" Melissa cried.

Sean shook his head. "I guess they'll do anything for a story."

DINGDONG! DINGDONG!

At the sound of the doorbell, Slobs began to howl. *"AROOOOOOOOOOO!"*

DINGDONG! DINGDONG!

"Good grief!" Sean shouted as he rose from the bed and staggered toward the hallway. "What's their hurry?"

DINGDONG! DINGDONG!

He shuffled down the stairs. Melissa was right behind him, clutching her robe tightly as Sean opened the front door.

To their amazement, the yard was full of people. Weird people!

"Here they are!" someone shouted. "The kids who talked to the ghost!"

"We didn't talk—" Melissa began. But her words were drowned out by cheers and applause. Cameras clicked and flashes flashed. A dozen hands pushed pens and papers at them, hoping to get their autographs. Their encounter with the ghostly hot rod had made them celebrities.

"Who are you people?" Melissa shouted. "What do you want?"

A plump woman wearing makeup and a flowing robe pushed her way to the front and pulled a crystal ball from her huge handbag.

"I'm Sabrina Swoboda," she said in an eerie, singsong voice. "I've come to help you communicate with the beings from beyond." She reached into her handbag a second time and pulled out a book. "I'm also selling my brand-new paperback, *How to Communicate with the Spirit World*."

She turned to the crowd. "For today only, it's just $19.95!"

Suddenly Mrs. Tubbs was pushing Sabrina out of the way. "What a bunch of bunk!" she scoffed. "I'll tell you what this is all about. It's all about Elvis!"

"Elvis?" Sean laughed. "What does Elvis have to do—"

"Think about it," Mrs. Tubbs interrupted. "A '56 Chevy with flames on the sides? It's obviously some sort of communication from the King of Rock 'n' Roll!"

"She's right," shouted a chubby man with thick sideburns, a receding hairline, and a double chin. He also wore sunglasses and had a guitar slung around his neck. "Elvis is back!"

"Are . . . are you . . ." Melissa stammered, "are you Elvis?"

"Who, me? No, ma'am . . . but you might say that he and I are—" he looked to the sky and strummed a note on his guitar—"in tune with each other."

He thrust out his hand. "Al Wilson," he said. "President of the Society of People Who've Seen Elvis Presley at Kmart." He patted Mrs. Tubbs on the shoulder. "Hildagard's the president of the Midvale chapter. And she's doing a terrific job."

Mrs. Tubbs blushed at the compliment.

"Anyway," Wilson said, "Elvis appeared to me and told me to schedule a concert for Midvale City Park this evening at 5:30. I'm going to sing a duet with him." He strummed another chord on his guitar. "Well, maybe not really him. More like his ghost. By the way, you wanna buy a couple of T-shirts?"

He held up a white T-shirt with a picture of Elvis in his prime and the slogan *Elvis almost ran me down in a '56 Chevy.*

"Only $9.95."

"No, thanks," Sean and Melissa answered.

"How 'bout a bumper sticker, then? Only $4.95."

Sean and Melissa began backing away.

"Not to worry," he shrugged. "But don't you dare miss that concert tonight! Elvis is gonna let us know why he's come back!"

He stepped into the crowd and was immediately surrounded by people wanting to buy T-shirts and bumper stickers.

Next, a tall, distinguished-looking man in a business suit came forward and thrust his business card into Sean's hands.

It read *Dr. James Thompson . . . Professor of Parapsychology . . . Midvale Community College.*

"Parapsychology?" Sean asked. "What's that?"

"We investigate ghosts . . . psychic phenomena . . . that sort of thing." Thompson smiled and continued. "I'm not a nutcase," he said, nodding in the direction of Mrs. Tubbs and the others. "And I'm not trying to sell anything. But I do have a professional interest in what you saw. All I ask is a few minutes of your time."

"We'll call you," said Melissa as she and Sean headed back into the house. "We have to go now. Thanks for coming! It's been fun!"

Sean started to slam the door.

"Wait!" cried Sabrina Swoboda, the spirit medium. "I've just received a message from beyond!"

Melissa rolled her eyes. It was obviously another corny attempt to sell books.

But it didn't stop the woman from continuing. "You're supposed to go see someone named Doc," she cried. "It's important."

"Thank you," Sean said, shutting the door. Then turning to Melissa he asked, "How did she know about Doc?"

"I don't know," Melissa answered. "That's kind of—"

"Spooky?" Sean finished his sister's sentence.

She nodded. "I mean . . . there's no way she could have known about Doc. Is there?"

The two looked at each other. A strange chill started to creep up both of their spines.

5

Now, That's Speed Skating!

TUESDAY, 9:05 PDST

"Will you please hurry up in there!" Sean banged on the bathroom door. "I'd like to get to Doc's before midnight, if you don't mind!"

No response.

He shook his head and sighed loudly.

Bloodhounds, Inc. had solved several tough mysteries over the last few months. But even if he lived to be 120, Sean knew he'd never solve the mystery of why it took his sister sooooo long to get ready in the morning.

He pounded on the door again. "You need some help in there? You fall in or something?"

Finally the door swung open. "No, I did not fall in!" Melissa looked him up and down and shook her head.

"Maybe *you* don't care what you look like when you go out," she sniffed, "but I do!"

"What's wrong with the way I look?"

"Nothing. The only thing missing is a sign that says *Will Work for Food*."

"Hey!"

"It was bad enough that all those people saw me looking like a wreck this morning." She turned and scowled at her reflection in the mirror. "Now I can't seem to do a thing with my hair."

Sean wanted to say something smart but realized she'd probably lock herself back in the bathroom for another hour. So he tired another technique. "Well, sis," he smiled. "You look terrific to me!"

"Really?"

"Absolutely!" It wasn't exactly a lie, but it wasn't exactly the truth, either.

"Well," she said, smiling back, "in that case, I guess I'm ready to go."

Sean let out a sigh of relief. He'd have to try being nice more often.

"So what's the plan?" she asked.

"First, I thought we'd drop by the radio station and ask Dad if he can give us a few minutes of airtime so we can tell everyone that Rafael Ruelas misquoted us."

"Good idea. I just hope Jeremiah doesn't cause us any more trouble."

Sean looked at his watch.

"How about it, Jeremiah?" he asked. "Promise you'll behave?"

Nothing.

Sean shrugged. "I guess he's still out there somewhere. Anyway, after that, I thought we could stop by Doc's."

Melissa frowned as she picked up her Rollerblades and slung them over her shoulder. "You don't really think that lady had a message from beyond, do you?"

"Of course not!" he said as he went into his bedroom to get his skateboard. "But still, I can't help wondering how she knew about Doc's."

"Me too," Melissa said. "Things just keep getting weirder and weirder."

TUESDAY, 9:44 PDST

"Hey, guys, what's up?"

Herbie, the best (and only) engineer for KRZY, the radio station Dad owned, was sitting in the lobby when the kids arrived.

"We came by to talk to Dad," Sean answered. "Why aren't you in the control room?"

Herbie smiled sheepishly and held up two heavily

bandaged hands. "Had a little accident," he said.

That wasn't surprising. Herbie was what you might call a little accident-prone. Well, actually, he was *a lot* accident-prone. What else could you call someone who had missed a week of work because he had a bowling ball stuck on his hand? Who once got his nose caught in a pencil sharpener?

"What happened this time?" Melissa asked.

"Toaster."

"Toaster? How could you—"

"Don't ask. But if you ever get some toast stuck in there . . ."

"Yeah?"

"Don't try to pull it out with your fingers."

"You put your hands down a hot toaster!"

"Don't be silly," Herbie said. "Only one of them. Got the other one caught in the food processor."

He waved one of his mitts in the direction of the control room. "Your dad's in there."

Melissa glanced up at the On the Air light, which burned brightly. "Okay if we go in?"

Herbie glanced at his watch. "Sure. It's just the *Cooking With Carol* show."

When they entered, Dad was sitting at the control panel, sipping a cup of coffee.

"Hey, guys, how's it going?"

"Oh, we're—" Sean began, and then stopped in midsentence as he looked through the soundproof window into the studio. "Is that Bear in there?"

"Yeah, that's Bear," Dad said. "And a couple of his friends."

Sure enough, there was Spalding, the rich kid who had called them earlier, and KC, a tomboy girl who gave the word *tough* a new meaning. And finally there was Bear—whose real name was Walter—a big, strong boy who loved to eat and sleep. Actually, sleep and eat. And when it came to smarts—well, let's just say he wasn't the brightest bulb in the pack.

"What's he doing in there?" Melissa asked. "And where's Carol?" (Carol Rawson had hosted Midvale's cooking show for just a little longer than anyone could remember.)

"Carol's on vacation," Dad said. "So we've been asking some of Midvale's best cooks to come on the show and give their favorite recipes."

"But . . . Bear?" Sean shook his head in disbelief.

"His banana pops won a blue ribbon at the county fair," Melissa reminded him.

"That's right," Dad nodded. "Bear wants to be a chef when he grows up, and I think he'll be a great one."

"It figures," Sean said, noticing that Bear had put on

59

another few pounds since they'd last seen him . . . a couple of days ago.

"And so," Bear was speaking over the microphone, "you take a yellow, ripe, beautiful banana . . . Spalding, would you please hand me one of those bananas?"

"Why, I'd be delighted to, Bear, my friend! Here it is!"

"Thank you, Spalding. And then you dip it in honey. KC, please bring me that jar of honey."

"Yeah, whatever!" her gravelly voice bellowed. It was so loud that Dad lunged for the volume control to turn it down. Unfortunately, Herbie had recently rewired and fixed the control board (which meant it wasn't fixed at all), and by turning the knob, Dad suddenly shorted out the entire board.

K-ZZZZZAP
POW!

The lights flickered, and the sound went dead.

"Hey, duds! I'm back!" said a small electronic voice. Apparently, the sudden shorting-out had brought Jeremiah back from hyperspace.

Meanwhile, in the studio, Bear placed the banana on a stick, dipped it in honey, and was preparing to roll it in a mixture of chopped nuts. "The next thing I do," he said, "is take the banana and roll it in . . ."

Dad grabbed the volume control knob again, this

time to turn it up. Another mistake.

K-BLOOEY!

Again the lights flickered, again the sound went dead, and again Jeremiah took off for parts unknown!

" . . . sawdust," Bear said.

Only it wasn't Bear! Somehow, KRZY had crossed lines with another radio station. A radio station where Mr. Fix-It was telling everyone how to get oil stains off of a driveway!

As Bear rolled his prizewinning bananas in chopped nuts, the voice going out over KRZY said, "And if sawdust doesn't work for you, you might give kitty litter a try."

All over Midvale, listeners of the *Cooking With Carol* show scratched their heads, double-checking their recipes. Dipping the bananas in honey was fine, but rolling them in sawdust or kitty litter was another matter.

Frantically, Dad worked the controls, trying his best to get Bear and the others back. But it was no use.

"And I find that a splash of acid can really work wonders," Mr. Fix-It was saying. "Just be sure you're wearing rubber gloves . . . because believe me, you don't want to get any acid on your fingers!"

Melissa whispered to her brother, "Maybe we should go."

"Wait a minute," Sean said. "I've got an idea." He turned toward their father. "Hey, Dad, I was just wondering if you could double my allowance?"

But Dad was so busy that he didn't really hear what Sean had said. "Huh?" he asked. "Oh yeah, sure . . . whatever."

"Sean!" Melissa scolded. "This isn't the time for—"

"Can you tell me a better time?" he said, flashing her a grin. He turned back to his father. "Dad, how about *tripling* that allowance?"

"Uh, I . . . sure, I guess."

"We gotta go, Dad," Melissa interrupted, giving her brother a stern look. "Right now!"

As she grabbed Sean's hand and pulled him out of the door, she whispered, "You ought to be ashamed of yourself."

"Hey," he complained, "you can't blame a guy for trying. . . ."

TUESDAY, 10: 32 PDST

As usual, the kids found their inventor friend, Doc, busy in her laboratory. She was *always* busy in her laboratory.

Doc was deaf and couldn't speak . . . so when she had something to say, she either used sign language or typed

62

it out on one of the computer keyboards she kept close at hand. To say that Doc was smart would be like saying the sun is warm. As far as Sean and Melissa figured, she was the most brilliant person in Midvale . . . probably the whole country!

Did you want to see us? Melissa signed.

I certainly did, Doc signed back.

Sean and Melissa looked at each other in surprise. The spirit lady had been right.

Doc stepped to her keyboard and typed, *I've got something exciting to show you!*

She pointed at a small object that looked like a pencil sharpener sitting on her workbench.

So what do you think? she typed.

Sean shrugged and signed, *What is it?*

It's a jet engine. It runs on a mixture of baking soda and lemon juice.

"A jet engine!" Sean exclaimed. "Wow! I wonder how this thing would work on my skate—"

"Sean!" Melissa cautioned. "Don't do anything stupid!"

Can I give it a try? he signed to Doc.

Well, I'm not sure it's ready to . . .

Thanks! He grabbed the tiny engine, then ran downstairs and out onto the porch where he'd left his skateboard.

Melissa followed right behind. "Sean, you know what always happens when you—"

"What could possibly happen?" he asked as he attached the little engine to his skateboard.

"Well, for one thing—"

VA-ROOOM!

The engine roared to life. Sean hopped on his skateboard, and before he knew it, he was racing off down the street.

"YOU DON'T KNOW HOW TO STOP IT!" Melissa finished, yelling her sentence.

"What?" Sean shouted back. He looked over his shoulder and saw his sister quickly disappearing into the distance. She was still yelling, but he couldn't hear. *Oh well*, he figured. *It's probably nothing important. After all, she's just my sister.*

The ride was great. Soon he was doing seventy-five . . . eighty miles an hour. Houses whizzed by. Picket fences became a blur. Lawns turned to swishes of green.

Then Main Street came into view, and it was time to put on the brakes. That's when it hit him: *What brakes?! How do I stop this thing?*

And what is that crossing the street up ahead? A marching band? Oh no! The Midvale Summer Festival starts today.

"Get out of the way!" he shouted. "Get out of the way!!"

But it did no good. No one heard him. Until, at the last second, a trombone player spotted him barreling down on them and screamed. Soon everyone was screaming and scrambling for safety. Woodwinds ran to the right! Brass to the left! Drums to the . . .

Well, it didn't look too good for the drum section.

KA-BOOM!

Sean bounced off the kettledrum, and . . .

RAT-A-TAT-TAT!

. . . his skateboard ricocheted off the snare as . . .

BOOM-SMASH!

. . . he went flying headfirst, right through the bass drum! It's a good thing that drum slowed him down. Otherwise, the tuba that he hit next might have killed him.

OOM-PAH! OOM-PAH!
OOM-KRASH!

He only saw it for a second before everything went dark!

Now he lay in the middle of the street with that stupid tuba stuck on his head! How embarrassing!

VAROOM! VAROOM!

Wait a minute! What was that? It wasn't the jet engine. It was something else. With more than a little effort, Sean managed to pull the tuba off his head.

KER-PLOP!

And just in time. For there, coming straight at him, was the red '56 Chevy! Maybe the tuba hadn't killed him, but now it looked like he was going to be a goner for sure.

He closed his eyes, waiting for the collision.

6

Roadkill on the Highway of Life

TUESDAY, 11:40 PDST

Every muscle in Sean's body tightened as the hot rod roared over him.

The sound of the engine was deafening.

He could even feel the heat from the big machine above him!

Somebody screamed. And then . . .

SILENCE.

He opened his eyes. There was no sign of the hot rod anywhere. It had disappeared without a trace!

All around him, dozens of band members and parade spectators stood frozen. They were so shaken by what they had seen that they couldn't move.

A moment later, Melissa was kneeling beside him,

tears streaming down her face. "Sean," she blubbered. "I thought you were dead! Are you all right?"

"I . . . I think so," he said, rising shakily to his feet.

The crowd slowly came back to life.

"Did you see that?" someone shouted.

"Yeah!" another yelled back. "That kid went plum through the bass drum! Strangest thing I ever saw!"

"No, not that! The car!"

"Oh, right! Disappeared like that! Second strangest thing I ever saw!"

Immediately, Melissa and Sean were surrounded by band members wanting to know if he was all right (and where they should send the bills so he could pay for the damaged drums).

"Here," Melissa said, handing Sean his skateboard.

"Oh, thanks." He took it and unhooked the little jet engine. "I guess you were right. I wasn't quite ready for this."

"Neither were your pants," she said, looking down at bloodstained knees, which poked through his tattered jeans.

Sean handed her the little engine. "Can you put this in your pocket?"

"Me? Why can't you put it in your pocket?"

"What pocket?" he asked.

She looked, and sure enough, there were only gaping

holes where his pockets used to be.

"Oh, all right," she said. "I suppose we better get those knees cleaned up and bandaged."

Sean nodded, and leaning on his sister for support, he slowly hobbled off in the direction of home. Sometimes little sisters weren't such a bother after all.

TUESDAY, 12: 21 PDST

"Here they come!"

"The chosen ones!"

"Hurrah!"

A crowd of at least one hundred people were milling around in Sean and Melissa's front yard. When they saw the kids approach, they burst into loud applause.

"What do you suppose this is all about?" Melissa whispered.

"I don't know, but I'll bet it has something to do with—"

"Rafael Ruelas!" Melissa exclaimed.

As if on cue, Ruelas stepped out of the crowd, microphone in hand. Walking beside the reporter was Sabrina Swoboda—the spirit medium. She held a large crystal ball.

Melissa noticed Ruelas and his crew were using the same old, frayed electrical cable they had used at the police station. Someone had tried to patch the damage with tape, but they hadn't done a very good job.

Uh-oh, she thought, *I hope we don't have more trouble with Jeremiah.*

"Here they are, ladies and gentlemen!" Ruelas shouted. "The two youngsters who, according to renowned medium Sabrina Swoboda, are the focus of the spiritual energy that has been unleashed on the citizens of Midvale."

More applause and whistling from the crowd.

Ruelas stuck his microphone in Sabrina's face.

"That's right, Rafael," the lady shouted. "These two youngsters are the focus of the spiritual energy that has been unleashed on the citizens of Midvale."

"Brilliant," Ruelas said. "Just brilliant. I couldn't have said it better myself!"

He shoved his microphone into Sean's face. "What do you have to say about that?" he asked.

"Like we told you before, we don't believe in—"

Ruelas pulled the microphone back. "That's great!" he shouted. "And what about you?" He turned to Melissa.

"I . . ."

Once again, he pulled the microphone away. "Exactly!"

He turned his attention back to the spirit medium.

"So, Sabrina . . . explain to our viewers what they're about to see."

"Well, Rafael, before we do that, I'd like to remind everyone that my new book, *How to Communicate with the Spirit World,* is available for a limited time only for just $21.95. Call 1-800 . . ."

"It was $19.95 this morning," Sean whispered.

"That was before she became a star," Melissa said. "If this keeps up, it'll be on sale for $99 before long."

"You really need to order one of these books today," Sabrina said. "It's a $99 value for only $25.95!"

Melissa gently nudged her brother. "What did I tell you?"

"That's wonderful, Sabrina," Ruelas said. "Of course, I haven't read your book . . . but I'm sure it's just tremendous. Now," he swept his hand toward Sean and Melissa, "tell us why these kids are so important to your work here in Midvale."

"These two are giving off tremendous amounts of spiritual energy," she replied. "That will make it easier for me to contact the creature from beyond who's been terrorizing Midvale in the ghost car."

She held the crystal ball in front of her, stared into it, and began moaning and groaning.

"Oooooh. Aaaaaah. Come, spirit, come!"

Melissa shook her head in disgust. "I've been trying

to tell you that we don't believe—"

"Aoooooh! The entity is approaching!"

Suddenly Sabrina's expression changed. She seemed startled. "I . . . I really do see something in there!" she shrieked.

"Of course you do," Ruelas encouraged her. "Why don't you tell our audience exactly what you see."

"He has red hair. Green skin . . ."

"Oh no!" Sean whispered to his sister.

"What?" she whispered back.

"I just remembered . . . crystal conducts electricity."
"So?"

"So if Jeremiah lives in electrical fields . . ."

Melissa got the point. "Uh-oh . . ."

"Double uh-oh!" Sean said, pointing to wispy gray smoke coming out of one of the electrical cords. "It's another electrical cable shorting out!"

"Uh . . . Mr. Ruelas," Sean called out, "You've got a little problem here!"

But Ruelas was too busy listening to the spirit medium.

The cord began to spark and hiss.

"No, wait a minute," Sabrina was saying. "His skin isn't green, it's blue. No, purple! And his eyes are glowing!"

No doubt about it. She was definitely describing Jeremiah!

SSSSSSSSSS. . . .

"It's horrible!" she screamed. "He's hideous! He's not a ghost! He's a monster! A demon!"

She thrust the crystal ball into Ruelas's hands and backed away. "Here! You take it! I don't want anything to do with it!"

SSSSSSSSSSSSSSSS . . .
KA-POW!

A loud boom! A flash of light . . . and suddenly Jeremiah was standing before them again, even bigger and scarier than when he'd been in the police station.

The crowd panicked and began running in all directions.

"EEAAGH!"

"Let me out of here!"

"Get out of my way!"

Jeremiah panicked, too. Something about being in the middle of a hysterically screaming mob will do that to a person. Quickly, he disappeared.

Sean looked around, then breathed a sigh of relief. "Thank you, Jeremiah," he whispered. "Thank you so very much."

"Yeah," Melissa nodded. "Maybe now we can get some detective work done!"

TUESDAY, 12:38 PDST

As soon as they got Sean's knees bandaged up, the two detectives headed back to Mrs. Sanks's neighborhood to look for clues. Several people had reported seeing the ghostly car in the area, and Sean and Melissa were hoping for some fresh evidence.

Sure enough, a few hundred yards down the road from the mansion's front driveway, Melissa spotted what looked like brand-new skid marks, as well as a few drops of oil in the road.

Sean scraped up some of the oil with his finger and held it out in front of Slobs.

SNIFF! SNIFF! SNIFF!

"You got it?" Sean said. "That's the scent, girl! Now . . . follow that car!"

"WOOF! WOOF!"

Slobs picked up the scent on the asphalt and began following it. She moved so fast, the kids had trouble keeping up.

And then, suddenly, she came to a screeching halt, stopping dead in her tracks.

"What is it, girl?" Melissa asked. "What do you see?"

As before, Slobs began to whine.

"She doesn't see anything," Sean said. "She's lost the scent . . . again!"

"But how could she? That's twice now."

"I don't know."

Sean bent down and picked up a piece of something lying in the road.

"What's that?" Melissa asked.

"I'm not sure." He held it out for her to see. "Some sort of metal, I think. But I've never seen anything quite like it."

"Wow! Look how shiny it is," Melissa said.

"Yeah. If you turn it just right, it's almost like . . ."

"A mirror?"

"Yeah . . . a mirror."

"Having any luck?" someone called out from behind them.

Sean turned and found himself looking into the face of Dr. James Thompson, the professor of parapsychology who had given them his business card earlier.

"Oh, hi," Sean said. "Nah . . . we're not really finding anything."

"I guess it's kind of hard to look for clues when that reporter won't leave you alone," the professor said.

"You can say that again," Melissa sighed.

"I blame that phony medium and her parlor tricks as much as I blame him," the professor said. He shook his head. "It's people like her that make my work so difficult."

"What do you mean?" Sean asked.

"I spend a lot of my time chasing ghosts," he said. "And they almost always turn out to be phonies . . . tricks played by charlatans like her. If people like that would quit wasting my time, maybe I could find out what's really going on out there."

He shook his head, then went on. "That's really why I came over here today."

"Why's that?" Melissa asked.

"I was on my way to Mrs. Sanks's house to ask if she would let me set up some of my equipment in her house."

"What kind of equipment?"

"I have some negative-ion oscillators and an audiovisual carbon-driven capacitor and—" He stopped in midsentence when he saw the puzzled look on Melissa's face.

"Go on," Sean said, pretending to know what he was talking about but obviously not having a clue. "I'm with you."

"What I mean is that I have some pretty sensitive audio and video equipment that can measure psychic impulses. If I could set up in Mrs. Sanks's living room,

then maybe I could find out what's really going on. Say
. . . maybe you could ask her for me. You seem to know
her pretty well."

"I don't suppose that would be a problem," Sean said.
"Whaddaya think, Misty?"

"I don't know," she said. "We really don't believe in
ghosts and—"

BRRRT! BRRRT!

Sean's cell phone began to chirp.

"Bloodhounds, Incorporated," he answered.

Widow Sanks's agitated voice came through the line.
"Something terrible has happened!" she cried. "Please . . .
come! Right away, you must come!"

7

Elvis, Is That You?

TUESDAY, 12:47 PDST

Five minutes later—thanks to a quick ride in the professor's beat-up Buick—Sean, Melissa, Slobs, and Professor Thompson stood on Mrs. Sanks's front porch as Sean rang her doorbell.

They heard the chimes ringing deep inside her house, but no one came to the door.

Sean rang the bell again, but there was only silence.

"What if something happened to her?" Melissa worried.

Almost immediately, they heard footsteps approach. The big front door creaked open, revealing Gretchen, Mrs. Sanks's personal nurse.

"Well, hello there," she said. "Mrs. Sanks is waiting for you in the parlor."

As they walked through the door, Sean glanced at his sister, trying not to laugh.

"What's so funny?" she asked.

"Your hair," he smirked. "It's standing straight up!"

"My hair!" She quickly tried to smooth it with her hands, until she looked at him and broke out laughing.

"What are you laughing at?" he asked.

"Your hair's standing up, too!" she giggled.

"It's happening to all of us," Professor Thompson said. "There's some kind of energy in this house."

"This has been going on for quite a while now," Nurse Gretchen assured them. "We've all become quite accustomed to it."

She led them down one hallway, then another, and another after that. Just when they were beginning to think they'd never be able to find their way out of the house again, they passed through a doorway and found themselves in a spacious drawing room full of elegant antique furniture.

Mrs. Sanks sat in a rocking chair in the corner. She looked strangely calm and peaceful, especially in light of the frantic phone call she had just made.

"Mrs. Sanks, are you all right?" Melissa asked.

"Why, yes, dear, I'm fine." She picked up a silver teapot and a delicate china cup from a table next to her. "You will join me for a spot of tea, won't you?"

"But, Mrs. Sanks," Sean sputtered. "We thought something terrible had happened."

"Oh, it has," she said as she handed Melissa a cup full of steaming tea. "And I'll tell you all about it later—after teatime."

"Mrs. Sanks never misses teatime," Gretchen explained. She turned toward the woman. "Will you be needing me for anything else?"

"No, Gretchen, thank you. You may go."

She nodded and walked out of the room.

"Mrs. Sanks," Sean said, "this is Professor Thompson. He teaches at the local college."

"Pleased to meet you, Dr. Thompson." She held out a cup of tea. "One lump or two?"

Twenty minutes later, after they'd consumed their tea and eaten at least a dozen tasteless cookies, she was ready to tell them about the horrible thing that had happened to her.

"Last night there were strange noises in the house," she began. "Doors opening and closing. Footsteps in the hall . . . but when I went to look, nobody was there."

"Go on," Sean said.

"Then this morning, my sweater was gone."

"Your sweater?" Melissa asked.

"My favorite one. It's white with blue flowers and a little pink—"

"Maybe you just forgot where you put it," Sean interrupted.

She shook her head. "It was hanging on the hook on my bedroom door. That's where I always put it. Somebody came into the house and took it. Maybe it was my son. Maybe he wants me to know he's here."

"But, Mrs. Sanks, just because your sweater is missing doesn't mean you're being visited by a ghost," Melissa said.

"That's right," Sean agreed. "There's bound to be a natural explanation. There's no such thing as ghosts."

He looked over at Melissa, whose hair was still standing up despite her best efforts to keep it under control.

At least, I hope there's no such thing as ghosts, he thought.

"Excuse me. Is this what you're looking for?"

Nurse Gretchen stood in the doorway, holding a white sweater with blue flowers and pink trim.

"Why, yes!" Mrs. Sanks's eyes opened wide in surprise. "Where did you find it?"

"In the oven."

"The oven?" Mrs. Sanks slowly made her way across the room to get a better look. "What was it doing in the oven?"

"I think maybe you put it there," Gretchen said as she

81

helped her employer into the sweater.

"But why would I do something like that?" the widow asked as she headed back across the room to her rocking chair.

"Who knows?" Gretchen shrugged. Then she whispered to the kids, "Mrs. Sanks has been a little confused lately. She's been hiding things in strange places. Last week, she put all the silverware in the washing machine. Then she took a half gallon of ice cream out of the freezer and put it in the dryer." She shook her head. "What a mess that was!"

"But what would make her do stuff like that?" Melissa whispered.

Gretchen shrugged. "Who knows? But if you ask me, this ghostly hot rod stuff is nothing more than her mind playing tricks on her."

"But we saw it, too," Sean reminded her.

"Did you, now?" the nurse asked. Her tone said she didn't really believe it.

Professor Thompson, who had been sitting quietly during all of this, turned toward Mrs. Sanks. "Would you mind if I set up some of my electronic equipment in your house?" he asked.

"I don't know. What kind of equipment? Why?"

"To help me figure out what's really going on around here," he said.

TUESDAY, 16:15 PDST

BEEP! BIP! BOOP!

Mrs. Sanks's living room was piled high with electronic gizmos, gadgets, and doohickeys. Over in one corner, a black box made a soft whirring sound. In another, a brown one beeped every few seconds. And on top of it sat a tiny radar dish, slowly revolving, looking for signals from who-knows-where.

"What's this thing?" Sean asked, tapping a glowing plastic cylinder with his finger.

"Don't touch that!" the professor warned. "It's an ectoplasm detector, and it's very sensitive."

"An ecto-what?"

"Ectoplasm detector. Ectoplasm is what ghosts are made of."

Sean and Melissa exchanged looks. They did not like the idea of this man believing in ghosts, no matter how nice he was.

The professor stepped back and admired his blinking, flashing, beeping machinery. "You're looking at the best collection of ghost-detection equipment this side of the Mississippi," he said proudly. "If there's a ghost lurking around here . . . this'll force him to show himself."

He pointed to a small TV monitor. "And when he does . . . we'll be able to see it right here."

"So what do we do now?" Melissa asked.

"Just sit back and let the fun begin," the professor answered.

"Fun?" she repeated.

"Like I said, if something supernatural is going on, we're going to know about it pretty quickly."

He produced a notepad and pen from his shirt pocket. Next, he pulled a chair up to his ghost-busting equipment so he could keep a close watch on the various dials and controls.

Sean made himself comfortable on the floor, and Melissa settled back on the couch. Both of them stared at the little monitor, which popped and sizzled with gray static.

Why should I be nervous? Melissa asked herself. *I don't even believe in ghosts.*

She continued to stare at the screen.

Still nothing but static.

She blinked.

More static.

She blinked again.

More.

BRRRRT! BRRRRT!

She jumped, startled by the sound of Sean's cell phone ringing.

Sean picked it up and answered, "Bloodhounds, Incorporated." He paused a moment, then answered, "Right, Mrs. Tubbs, thanks for reminding us. No, we wouldn't miss it for the world. Thanks for calling!"

He clicked it off.

"So what did Mrs. Tubbs want?"

"To remind us that the Elvis concert starts in an hour."

"You really think we ought to waste our time?"

"A good detective can't afford to overlook any clues," he reminded her. "Mrs. Tubbs says something very important is going to happen there, so we should probably check it out."

He turned to the professor. "Will you let us know if anything happens here?"

Dr. Thompson looked up from his pen and paper.

"Got your number right here. I'll call you the minute anything happens."

"Great!"

Sean checked his watch. "We'd better head on over to the park."

TUESDAY, 17:18 PDST

The park was packed. And at least half of the people were dressed like Elvis—slicked-back hair, bushy sideburns, sunglasses, and lots and lots of leather.

"Hey," a familiar voice called out, "wanna buy a banana pop?"

Bear, KC, and Spalding stood behind the counter of a little refreshment stand.

"Hey, guys, what's up?" Sean asked.

"What's up," Spalding said, "is that I've decided to bankroll Bear's little business here. I get half of all the profits. That means I get a dollar for every banana pop he sells."

"And I get a whole dime!" Bear chimed in.

Spalding nodded his head. "That's right, Bear. You get a whole dime." He smiled. "As you can see, he's a terrific business partner."

It looked like Spalding and Bear had hit upon a great idea. People were lining up to try the tasty new treat. One man plunked his cash on the counter, unwrapped a banana pop, and took a big bite.

One of the Elvis wanna-bes was next.

"How much are they?"

"Two dollars," Spalding replied.

The man reached into his billfold for some money

when a very disturbing look crossed his face. "Say, these aren't those banana pops I heard about on KRZY, are they?" he asked.

"That's right," Spalding said proudly.

"Then forget it!" he exclaimed. "I can't believe you roll these things in kitty litter!"

"*HAACK! HAACK!*" The woman standing next to him suddenly began to cough. The half-chewed piece of banana shot out of her mouth like a rocket and struck Spalding between the eyes, where it stuck.

"Kitty litter!" someone said.

"They've gotta be nuts!" another exclaimed.

"I'm outa here!"

"We're all outa here!" others in the group agreed.

"No! Wait!" cried Spalding. "It's not true!"

But it was too late. His business was gone before it even had a chance to get started.

Sean clapped his hands over his ears.

What was that horrible sound?

Cats yowling on a back fence? Someone scraping his fingers across a chalkboard?

There it was again! It was coming from the other side of the park.

"We'd better hurry!" Melissa shouted. "Sounds like someone's screaming for help!"

With Slobs leading the way, Sean and Melissa quickly pushed through the crowd, moving toward the strange noise, which grew louder and more frightening.

Finally, they came into a large clearing and found themselves in front of the park's bandstand.

Up on the stage, Elvis impersonator Al Wilson was banging on a guitar and trying to sing. Only it was obvious he didn't know how to do either.

Slobs threw back her head and howled. "AROOOOOOOOOOOOOO!" She sounded more like Elvis than Wilson.

" 'Don't be cruel,' " Wilson screeched, launching into one of Elvis's best-known hits. Speaking of cruel, it was unlikely anyone had ever been so cruel to one of Elvis Presley's songs.

But Wilson continued strumming his guitar and swiveling. He moved like someone who was being poked with an electric cattle prod.

"AROOOOOOOOOOOO!" Slobs howled again and tried to cover her sensitive ears with her paws.

All over the park, people began moving away, trying desperately to escape the ear-shattering torture of Wilson's "singing."

But Sean was surprised to see that someone really

seemed to be enjoying his act. She was dancing, snapping her fingers, and singing along. On the ground next to her sat a fat cat dressed up like a little Elvis—with sunglasses perched on his face and a tiny guitar hanging from his neck.

"Hi, Mrs. Tubbs," Sean shouted over the racket. "Looks like you and Precious are really enjoying this!"

"Oh yes! He's great, isn't he?"

Sean didn't want to tell a lie, so he just smiled.

"Thank you very much! Thank you!" At long last, Wilson's song was finished, and he was bowing and thanking the dwindling crowd for their applause. But, of course, there was no applause. There was barely an audience.

"Now, don't forget, folks," Wilson said, "I have Elvis T-shirts, CDs, and bumper stickers on sale. And every bit of the money goes to my favorite charity—me! Now, for my next number—"

"Hold on!" shouted a big, bearded biker in a leather jacket. "You promised you were going to reveal some great secret about Elvis and that ghost car!"

"That's right!" agreed a little old lady with purple hair.

A chorus of similar cries went up from the group.

"Well," Wilson cleared his throat, "you see . . . uh. . . . the truth is that Elvis never died. Yeah . . . that's it. He just . . . ascended into a higher state of being. And if everyone will believe real hard, then maybe—"

He stopped in midsentence, and a stunned look filled his face. "Holy mackerel!" he yelled. "Here he comes now!" He gestured to an area just beyond the crowd.

Twenty-five heads turned to see what he was pointing at.

VAROOOOM! VAROOOOM!

As if on cue, the ghostly hot rod suddenly appeared in the distance, roaring down the small street that dead-ended into the park.

A loud gasp went up from the crowd.

Maybe Elvis was driving that car, and maybe he wasn't. But whoever it was, he was heading straight for the crowd!

8

Burnin' Rubber!

The phantom car reached the end of the street but then kept on coming! It jumped the curb, broke through a chain link fence, and roared into the park.

"Look out!" Sean shouted. He pushed Melissa to the ground and fell on top of her to protect her as the big car whizzed past, so close the breeze blew Sean's hair.

People all around were screaming and diving for cover.

KER-SMASH!

There went a picnic table.

K-RUNCH!

A barbecue grill was next.

K-POW!

That had been the teeter-totter.

And still the phantom car didn't slow down. With thick black smoke pouring out of its twin exhausts, it raced right through the park and onto the street at the other end, where it disappeared from view.

"Misty, are you okay?" Sean asked as he helped his sister to her feet.

She spit a few blades of grass from her mouth and brushed the dirt from her pants. "I'm okay," she whined, "but I don't know if I'll ever be able to get these clean!"

All over the park, people were crawling out from under bushes and picnic tables. Fortunately, nobody seemed to be hurt. Just badly shaken.

Sean turned and looked toward the stage. Al Wilson was nowhere in sight. His guitar lay broken on the ground, as if he had dropped it and left the stage in too big of a hurry to pick it up.

"Come on," Sean said. "We've gotta find that Wilson guy and see what he knows about this."

Minutes later, they found him backstage, hurriedly throwing his things into an old, battered suitcase. His hands were shaking as he loaded the last of his bumper stickers.

"Are you leaving, Mr. Wilson?" Melissa asked.

He didn't answer. Instead, he dropped the final T-shirts into the suitcase and snapped it shut.

"Mr. Wilson, what's going on?" Sean asked.

"I don't have the slightest idea!" he said. "Look! I just came to Midvale to see if I could make a few bucks. The Elvis stuff was all a joke."

"But the car . . ." Sean began.

Wilson shook his head. "I was just having a little fun. I never expected that car to show up."

He picked up the suitcase. "Now I just want to get out of town as fast as possible." With that, the Elvis impersonator strode away.

"So what should we do now?" Melissa asked.

BRRRRT! BRRRRT!

The cell phone.

"Bloodhounds, Incorporated," Sean answered.

Dad was on the other end. "Guys, I think you'll want to get down here to the station. Things are really hopping about that ghostly hot rod."

TUESDAY, 18:08 PDST

At the radio station, Dad was hosting a special edition of *Midvale On Line*, which invited listeners to call the station to talk about whatever was on their minds. He was working hard. His tie hung loosely around his neck, and his shirt sleeves were rolled up to the elbows. While he talked rapidly to a caller on one of the station's phone lines, two other lines blinked on hold, and one more rang loudly.

Herbie tried to help answer them, but with those big bandages on his hands, he kept hanging up on people by accident.

"Oops!" he said. "I just disconnected another one."

"Here, let us help," Melissa offered, reaching past him for the ringing phone. She punched the buttons for lines two and three. "KRZY . . . hold, please."

Sean grabbed the other phone. "KRZY . . . just a moment, please."

"Thanks, guys," Herbie said. "Those phones won't stop ringing tonight. Everybody wants to talk about that ghostly hot rod thing."

At the moment, Dad was finishing up his conversation with Chief Robertson.

". . . and that's why he's come back from the dead. To get revenge," the chief said. "I didn't want anyone to know about it, but seeing as how it's been all over the TV the past couple of days, I thought I ought to call and clear the air."

"Well, thank you for calling, Chief. Now let's see who's on line two."

He punched into another line. "Good evening, caller. You're on the air."

"Thank you for taking my call."

Melissa thought the voice sounded familiar. "I just wanted to say that the chief is a little confused, but he's on the right track."

"He is? And how do you know that?"

"I'd rather not talk about it over the air. But if any of your listeners really want to know what's going on in Midvale, I urge them to buy a copy of my new book. It's only $35.95, and they can get it by calling . . ."

Sabrina Swoboda! Melissa thought. No wonder the voice sounded familiar.

Realizing the woman was trying to sell something, Dad ended the call as gracefully as possible and picked up the next line. "KRZY . . . you're on the air."

"I was just wondering what you think about all this?" the caller asked. "What are your feelings about this ghostly hot rod business?"

"Well," Dad responded, "I really don't know what's going on in Midvale right now, but I'm pretty sure it doesn't have anything to do with a ghost."

Sean and Melissa paused to listen.

"After all," Dad continued, "the Bible says in the book of Hebrews that when a person dies, his soul goes to be judged by God, and then he either goes to heaven or hell. Now, there are spirits—the Bible calls them demons or fallen angels—but they are not the souls of dead people."

"I see."

"And while we're at it," Dad said, "the Bible also has some very strong warnings against people trying to contact the dead."

Melissa and Sean exchanged looks. It was obvious they were both proud of how much their dad knew.

"Well, thanks for calling," he said, pressing the button and going to the next call. "You're on the air."

"And you're nuts!" an angry voice shouted. "The truth is Midvale is under attack from this ghost. And we'd better find out what he wants and give it to him before he hurts somebody."

CLICK! The caller hung up loudly, but Dad didn't miss a beat. "And we'll be back to take more of your calls right after this short commercial break." He motioned to Herbie, who hit a switch, and a commercial for Ralph's Truck Stop and Diner was on the air.

"And I want all you good people of Midvale to come on down to Ralph's," a voice was saying. "Come on down to eat some dinner and get lots of gas!"

As the commercial played, Dad leaned back, removed his earphones, and sighed. "This is turning out to be a really weird night," he said.

"Yeah," Sean agreed. "Something is definitely going on out there."

Dad rested his chin in his hand and thought for a moment. "Sometimes, I wonder if people's minds are just playing tricks on them," he said.

"But we've seen it with our own eyes!" Melissa protested.

"I know you have," Dad nodded. "But it's possible to see all kinds of things that aren't really there. Especially when other people think they're seeing them, too. It's called the power of suggestion."

"This thing isn't powered by suggestion," Sean argued. "It's got a great big '56 Chevrolet engine."

Dad laughed. "Oh, I almost forgot," he said. "Did you guys get my message about Doc?"

"What message?" Melissa asked.

"I got a call yesterday that Doc wanted to see you guys about something. I wrote it down on a piece of paper just as I was running out the door to work. But I really don't remember what I did with it."

Sean and Melissa exchanged knowing glances. So that was how Sabrina Swoboda knew Doc wanted to see them. Dad must have dropped that paper as he was going out the door. Some psychic she was!

Sean smiled at his sister. "See! I told you there's always a logical explanation."

"What was that?" Dad asked.

"He just means that we got the message," Melissa answered. "Thanks, Dad."

"Good." Dad looked at his watch and sighed. The commercial was almost over. It was time to get back to work.

BRRRT! BRRRT!

Sean's phone was at it again.

"Bloodhounds, Incorporated."

"EAGGHH! HELP ME!" And the phone went dead.

"Who was it?" Melissa asked.

"Grab your Rollerblades," Sean answered. "We've got to got to go see Mrs. Sanks right now! Dad . . ."

Dad waved his hand. "Don't give it another thought," he said. "If she's in trouble, you've got to go. We'll hold down the fort here."

TUESDAY, 18: 49 PDST

Nurse Gretchen met them at the front door of the widow's mansion. "Honestly, we don't know what happened," she said, dabbing at her eyes. "Everything was fine. And then she just started screaming and carrying on. We tried to get her calmed down. . . ."

Gretchen shook her head and bit her lip. "The professor is in there with her now."

Once again, the kids' hair began to stand up as they walked through the door. But this time they both tried to ignore it.

Mrs. Sanks was in her bedroom, lying on top of her bed while the professor fanned her face with an old magazine, trying to give her some air. When she saw the kids and Slobs, she tried to sit up, but Nurse Gretchen persuaded her to lie back down.

"I'm glad you're here," she said. "Horrible things happened while you were gone! Hands came out of the walls! I saw evil, glowing eyes looking in through the window! And I heard the most awful moaning and groaning!" She covered her face with her hands and began to cry.

"I thought my son was coming back," she sobbed. "But now I know something awful is going on here. And I'm scared! I'm so scared!"

"Now, now, Mrs. Sanks," her nurse said. "You've got to settle down. You know it's bad for your heart to get all worked up like this." Then she turned and whispered to the kids, "I'm going to give her a sedative. She's got to get some rest."

The professor motioned for the kids to join him in the hall.

"I wonder what he wants to talk to us about," Sean whispered as he and Melissa followed him out of the room.

Melissa shrugged as they entered the hall and walked just far enough away so Mrs. Sanks couldn't hear them.

The professor sighed, looked around to see if anyone else might be listening, and began. "I'm afraid the old woman must be out of her mind," he said, shaking his head. "Absolutely nothing unusual happened while you were gone. My equipment picked up no trace of anything out of the ordinary."

"But Mrs. Sanks said—" Melissa protested.

"Obviously, the poor lady is mentally deranged," he interrupted. "I think she needs to be in a psychiatric hospital. And frankly, I'm beginning to think that this whole ghostly hot rod business is nothing more than mass hysteria."

"But if you had seen what just happened in the park . . ." Sean argued.

"It's amazing what an entire group of people can see when they all believe the same thing," he said. "I visited a village in India once where the people believed they had seen an elephant flying. They hadn't, of course. But they believed so strongly, there was no convincing them otherwise."

"I don't know," Sean said. "It all seems so real."

Nurse Gretchen joined them in the hall, sadly shaking her head. Melissa's heart went out to the old lady. She was so sweet, so nice, and so vulnerable. "Would you mind if Sean and I sat with Mrs. Sanks awhile?" Melissa asked. "It might make her feel good just to know we're there with her."

"That would be nice," the nurse said.

"Well, I think I'd better get back to my equipment," the professor said. "Just in case."

TUESDAY, 19:18 PDST

The sedative worked quickly, and Mrs. Sanks was soon sleeping—but not soundly. She kept moaning and groaning in her dreams. Melissa felt terrible as she and Sean sat in nearby chairs. Suddenly they heard a familiar electronic voice.

"She's not crazy, you know," it said.

"Jeremiah!" Sean looked down at his watch. "Welcome back. I thought you were afraid."

"Not anymore," Jeremiah said. "I've come to the concussion that there is no ghost."

"Conclusion . . . not concussion," Melissa said. "But how did you figure that out?"

"It was easy as falling off a piece of cake," he replied. "There's something going on here, all right, but it's not supernatural. It's electrical. This house is producing way too much electricity. I can feel it in my circuitry."

"Yes!" Melissa cried. "That's why our hair stands up. There's some kind of electrical charge in the air!"

Sean rose to his feet and nodded in agreement. "It's like static electricity or something."

Jeremiah nodded. "And it's time we grabbed the bull by the tail and looked him in the eyes."

Melissa almost smiled. "Don't you mean—"

"Whatever," Sean interrupted. "But right now there's something else in the air that makes me want to sn . . . sn . . . sneeze. . . ."

Melissa turned back to Mrs. Sanks as Sean stumbled across the room, trying to fight off the sneeze building in his nose. But it was a losing battle!

AHHH . . . CHOOO!

"Bless you!" Melissa said.

There was no response. No thank-you. No wisecrack. No nothing.

"Sean?"

More of the same.

She turned back to her brother, but there was no sign of him anywhere. He was gone—vanished into thin air!

9

Sneeze the Day

TUESDAY, 19:25 PDST

"Sean!" Melissa called out. "Sean, where are you?"

She got down on the floor and looked under Mrs. Sanks's bed. "If you're trying to be funny, you'd better stop it right now!"

Nothing under the bed (but a few dust bunnies).

"Sean! I mean it!"

She stuck her head out in the hall, looking one way, then the other.

"Sean!"

The widow Sanks moaned softly in her sleep.

"Jeremiah," Melissa called softly. "Are you here?"

Silence.

"Okay, then," Melissa said to herself. "I guess it's time to call the police."

Sean stared into the darkness, trying to get his eyes to focus.

"W-w-what happened?" Jeremiah asked, his voice shaking with fright.

"I don't know," Sean whispered. "I hit something when I sneezed, and the next thing I knew, I was in here."

"But where is here?" Jeremiah asked.

"I don't know."

"And why are you whispering?"

"Because wherever we are, I have a feeling we're not supposed to be here."

Sean blinked hard and peered into the darkness. "I think we're in some kind of tunnel," he said. "I always heard that old houses like this are full of secret passageways."

Slowly, putting one foot in front of the other, Sean began making his way into the darkness.

"Where we going, dud?" Jeremiah asked.

Sean sighed. "Would you please try to remember that it's *dude* and not *dud*?"

"Sorry."

"I'm trying to find my way out of here."

"Well, remember," Jeremiah said, "when I'm in this watch of yours, wherever you go, I go. So please . . . be careful!"

Upstairs, Melissa was on the phone with the dispatcher from the Midvale Police Department. But she wasn't getting anywhere.

"Honey, are you sure your brother's not just playing a practical joke on you?"

"No, listen, he's disappeared, and I think he might be in trouble. You've got to help."

"I'm sorry, hon, but we can't do anything until he's been missing for at least twenty-four hours."

"Twenty-four hours! It could be too late by then!"

"I'm sorry. That's our policy."

"But you don't understand—"

"There's nothing we can do. Good-bye."

Sean stepped on a loose board in the dark and . . . "Oooof!" . . . stumbled against a wall.

It's so dark in here! he thought. *What's that up ahead? A flicker of light?*

Sean took a step closer.

Yes! There it is again! Maybe it's the way out of here!

As he made his way forward, it became more and more clear that there was a light up ahead. And it was blinking on and off, like a Christmas tree.

He rounded the corner and gasped. Because there, right in front of him, was . . .

THE GHOSTLY HOT ROD!

There was no mistaking the car. It had those huge flames down the sides. And there were fresh dents and scratches from its recent romp in the park.

Sean cautiously approached. He could still feel the heat coming off the engine. It hadn't been parked there very long. Just beyond it was a huge electrical generator, where dozens of lights blinked rapidly.

"Shazzaam!" Jeremiah exclaimed. "It's—"

"Shhhhhhhh!" Sean whispered. "I hear voices."

Melissa shook her head, picked up the phone, and punched the police number again.

"Midvale Police Department."

"May I speak to Chief Robertson, please?" she said, trying to sound very grown-up.

"He's in a meeting. Can someone else help you?"

"Would you please tell the chief I have to talk to him? It's very important."

"And who may I say is calling?"

"Tell him I'm calling for Willy Sanks," Melissa said.

There was a click, followed by a few moments of intercom music.

Finally the chief's voice came on the line. "Willy Sanks," he gasped. "He talked to you?"

"Uh . . . not exactly, Chief."

"What? Who is this? What's the meaning of this?"

"Chief . . . this is Melissa Hunter . . . and I'm inside the Sanks mansion."

"Yes?"

"Sean's disappeared!"

"Disappeared? You mean he—"

"Vanished. One minute he was here, and the next he was gone. I'm afraid something terrible has happened to him."

"Willy Sanks has got to be behind this," he said.

"But—"

"Trust me, I'm a professional, I know these things. And it's about time I confronted that ghost man to, er . . . I mean, man to . . . whatever. I'll be right over!"

107

The voices grew louder—coming from somewhere just beyond the wall. A moment later, Sean spotted a door. But it wasn't completely closed—it was open just a crack. He slowly approached it, hoping he could steal a peek and see what was going on.

Yes! Now he could see. It was Nurse Gretchen! And the professor! She was looking over some of his electronic equipment.

"That was so amazing!" she laughed. "How in the world did you get those hands to come out of the wall like that? And those eyes glowing in the dark? They seemed so real!"

"It's easy when you're an electronics genius," the professor chuckled. "Besides, that sort of thing is child's play next to my baby in there." He pointed toward Sean's door.

"You mean getting it to drive around with nobody in it?"

"Nah, that's a piece of cake. But learning how to make it disappear . . . that was the difficult part."

"And how do you do that?"

He brushed the question off with a wave of his hand. "You wouldn't understand. It's too complicated."

"Try me."

"Well . . . ahem," the professor cleared his throat, "how do I put it in layman's terms? Mostly, it's stealth technology I learned from the United States government. It has to do with a mirror coating directly underneath the outer paint job. When the car reaches seventy-five miles an hour, the molecules in the undercoating begin to vibrate at a frequency directly proportionate to the—"

"Can you give me the shorthand version?" Gretchen interrupted.

"Okay . . . at a certain rate of speed, the hot rod turns into a mirror. You can't see it because it's reflecting everything around it. And then, of course, there's its ability to become absolutely silent."

Gretchen nodded. "That's when you make those wings come out, lift off the ground, and silently glide through the air."

"That's right," he chuckled. "Then nobody can see or hear a thing. *Woosh . . .*" he whispered, moving his hand through the air, "just like a silent airplane."

So that's it! Sean thought. *No wonder Slobs lost the scent! Because the car lifted off into the air! And that's why it didn't hit me during the parade. It flew right over me!*

"You really are amazing," Gretchen laughed.

He smiled. "When you're right, you're right."

She shook her head and sighed. "Just think. Fifteen years I've served that woman for almost no pay, without so much as a thank-you. But as soon as we get her declared legally insane, everything she owns will belong to me."

"And me!" the professor reminded her.

"That's right, darling." She kissed him on the forehead. "And you . . . my brilliant little ghost-maker."

Now Sean understood. The ghost car was nothing but a trick to get the widow's money!

Once again Sean's nose twitched. Uh-oh. Something was in the air again, and a sneeze was building. The same sort of sneeze that had landed him in this secret passageway to begin with!

"Ah . . . ah . . . ah . . ."

"Don't dud it, do!" Jeremiah cried.

But it was too late!

AH-CHOOOOOOOO!

"What was that?" the nurse asked.

"Somebody's in the tunnel! Quick, turn off the light." Immediately the room went black.

"I'll bet it's those kids!" the nurse growled.

"Don't worry," the professor said, "I'll take care of them!"

10

Rocket Girl

TUESDAY, 19:45 PDST

Sean turned and began to run. But in the darkness, he made it only about four feet before stumbling and falling.

"Oaff!"

He staggered back to his feet, wondering, *Which way should I run?*

This way!

No . . . that way!

The door flew open, and he heard the professor enter the tunnel.

Once again, Sean ran into a wall and fell.

"Get up!" Jeremiah cried. "When the going gets tough, the tough get off their duff!"

Sean scrambled to his feet and took off in the darkness.

By now, Professor Thompson was right behind. But the man had the advantage because he knew the old tunnel like the back of his—

K-BAMB!

"Owwww!"

Well, maybe he didn't know it so well after all.

With the professor on the ground, this was Sean's chance to get away. He raced around the next corner and came face-to-face with . . .

. . . a dead end.

There was no escape. The professor was back on his feet and almost upon him.

Sean spun around. "I didn't hear a thing," he blurted out. "Really, I didn't."

The professor gave no answer. He just kept on coming. And in the dimmest of light, Sean could see an evil smile spread across the man's face.

Upstairs, in Mrs. Sanks's bedroom, Melissa slowly felt her way along the wall. She knew that it would take at least ten minutes for the police to arrive, and that might be ten minutes too late. She had to do everything she could now to save her brother's life.

"Maybe this is just like in the movies," she said to Slobs. "Maybe he touched something, and a trapdoor opened up. Whaddaya think, girl?"

"WOOF!"

"Come on over here and help me look."

Melissa felt her way all around the bookcase, the nightstand, and the bedposts. All of these seemed likely places to hide a secret switch. But if it was there, she couldn't find it.

Meanwhile, Slobs was sniffing her way along the other side of the room, but she wasn't finding anything, either.

"I don't understand," Melissa said. "He was right here. And the next moment—"

"My, but you're a nosy little thing, aren't you?"

Melissa spun around to see Nurse Gretchen standing in the doorway. The friendly smile she always wore was gone. Her soft, pleasant features had taken on a hard, menacing look.

"Oh, I'm sorry," Melissa said. "I didn't realize I was doing anything wrong."

"What exactly *were* you doing, snooping around like that?" The nurse took a step toward her but kept her right hand hidden behind her back.

"I was just . . . I was just . . ."

"I know what you were doing, you little brat!" she

113

said as she continued to approach. "You were spying on us, that's what you were doing! Trying to stop me from getting what I deserve for taking care of this silly old woman all these years. But it's not going to work!"

She suddenly produced her right hand, which held a huge hypodermic needle full of a cloudy greenish liquid.

"And you know *why* it's not going to work?" she said as she kept coming closer and closer. "Because I'm going to give you a shot that's going to make you sleep for a long, long time."

She lunged with the needle, but Melissa leaped aside. "Slobs!" she shouted. "Do something!"

"WOOF! WOOF!"

Thinking it was a game, the huge dog leaped on the woman's chest, accidentally sending her staggering across the room. As she put out her hand to keep from falling, she hit the wall just below the light switch and . . .

BINGO!

. . . the floor suddenly opened up beneath her.

"Eeeeaaah!" she screamed.

Then it closed back up and she was gone. And Slobs with her.

Before Melissa could react, she heard the sound of police sirens outside.

Inside the secret passageway, Sean and Professor Thompson heard the sirens, too!

"Oh, great!" the professor said. By now, he had grabbed Sean and was twisting the boy's arm behind his back. "I guess that stupid little sister of yours called the police!"

"Misty's not stupid!" Sean shouted.

"WOOF! WOOF!"

"Help!" It was Nurse Gretchen. She came running out of the darkness screaming, "Get this dog away from me!"

Slobs was right behind her, barking good-naturedly, obviously thinking the chase was part of the game.

"She bit me!" Gretchen screamed, grabbing her rear with her hand. "She bit me! She bit me!"

But as she came closer, Sean saw she wasn't suffering from a dog bite but a big hypodermic needle sticking out from the seat of her crisp white uniform. Apparently, when she fell through the trapdoor, it had jabbed into her. All of the liquid was still in the syringe, but it still must have hurt.

"What are you doing here?" the professor demanded.

"That little brat pushed me through the trapdoor!" she cried. "We've got to get out of here! These kids have ruined everything!"

"Call off your dog!" the professor commanded.

When Sean didn't respond, the professor twisted his arm even harder. "I said, *call off your dog!*"

"Okay, okay!" Sean cried. "Slobs . . . that's enough playing. Come here, girl."

Delighted to see her master, Slobs ran over to him, wagging her tail furiously.

"Good dog."

"What are we going to do?" Gretchen cried.

"We've got to make a break for it," the professor said as he gently removed the needle from his partner's posterior.

"But I—"

"They'll never be able to catch us," he said. "The car's too fast for them. We'll come back later and take care of that bratty girl."

They headed to the car. The professor ordered Sean into the backseat, and Slobs quickly followed, obviously thinking it was still part of the game.

The professor gestured for Gretchen to get into the front passenger's seat.

"But I—"

"No buts!" snapped the professor. "Let's go!"

"—get carsick!" she whined as she reluctantly climbed aboard.

Chief Robertson and a couple of his best men pounded on Mrs. Sanks's front door.

Melissa finally arrived, threw open the door, and shouted, "Follow me!"

She led them down the hallways and into Mrs. Sanks's bedroom, where the widow was still snoring loudly.

"Stand back!" She motioned them away. "It's a trapdoor!"

Suddenly Mrs. Sanks sat up. "Why, thank you! How nice of you to come!" she said, then fell back and continued snoring.

"Watch what happens when I do this!" Melissa said. She slapped the wall just below the light switch.

Nothing.

She slapped it again.

Still nothing.

"I don't know what you're trying to do, but let me take a crack at it," one of the officers said.

Apparently, the third time was the charm.

WHACK!

The floor opened up, and he tumbled into the secret

passageway below. "*AAEEAAGGHH!*"

"You're right!" shouted the chief. "It's a trapdoor. Come on, let's—" He stopped in midsentence. "Wait a minute! Listen!"

From deep beneath the house came the sound of an engine revving up. A very powerful engine!

"They've got a car in there!" the chief exclaimed.

"I'll bet it's the ghostly hot rod!" Melissa cried.

"They're trying to escape!" said the chief. "We'll never catch them on foot! We've gotta get back to the squad car!"

He stooped down and yelled into the trapdoor, "Chauncey, are you all right?"

"Fine, Chief" came the reply.

"We'll try to head 'em off at the pass!" the chief shouted.

The professor slammed the ghostly hot rod into gear, stomped on the accelerator, and the powerful car burned rubber as it took off, heading straight for . . .

. . . A BRICK WALL!

Sean covered his eyes! They were going to crash!

But at the last minute, the wall flew open and the car

was suddenly out of the tunnel and onto the road.

In the front seat, Nurse Gretchen's face was green, and she was gasping for breath.

"Can . . . you . . . please . . . slow down?" she coughed. "I'm gonna be . . . gonna be . . ."

The professor thrust a brown paper bag into her hands. "Here, use this."

" . . . sick."

BLEEAAGGHH!

Yuck! She wasn't kidding!

"Wait for me!" Melissa shouted as the chief and his partner ran ahead of her to their patrol car. But they weren't listening. Instead, the two men jumped into the car and took off, leaving her standing in the dust.

Melissa stomped her foot in anger. "Now what am I gonna do?"

That's when she saw her Rollerblades sitting on the widow's front porch. She felt in her pocket for Doc's tiny jet engine. Yes! It was still there!

She looked up to heaven. "God," she said, "please help me. I know this is gonna be dangerous . . . but I've got to do *something*!"

The ghostly hot rod rounded the corner, almost crashing into the side of the police car. It fish-tailed, swung hard to the right, and continued, just ahead of the car with its flashing lights and screaming siren.

"Don't worry," Professor Thompson shouted. "They'll never be able to catch us."

"BLEAAGGHH!" was all Gretchen could say in response.

Unfortunately, the professor was right. The police car was no match for the powerful hot rod. In less than a minute, the patrol car fell a hundred yards behind, and the gap grew wider every second.

Back in the police car, the chief shouted, "Can't you go faster?"

The driver shook his head. "I've got it floored, sir."

ROOOOOARRRR! WOOSH . . .

"Good grief!" the driver shouted. "What is that?" He pointed out his window, where something, or someone, was zipping past them as if they were standing still.

"It's Melissa!" shouted the chief. "On Rollerblades! And she's doing at least 120!"

"Don't look now!" Gretchen shouted. "But somebody's gaining on us!"

"Gaining on us! Who?" the professor demanded.

"It looks like . . . a girl . . . on Rollerblades!"

Sean turned to look over his shoulder. "Melissa!" he shouted. "Way to go, sis!"

"Do something!" Gretchen shouted.

A moment later and Melissa was at their side, banging on the window, then the door.

"Make us invisible!" Gretchen shouted. "Make us fly out of here!"

"I can't! It won't work when someone is touching the paint!"

Melissa continued banging on the door. She began shouting, "Pull over! Pull over!"

The hot rod's tires squealed as it made a sharp right turn onto Mill Road.

But somehow, Melissa hung on and managed to stay right with it.

Next came a hard left onto Wilson Street.

Melissa was still there, hanging on for dear life.

Then a right on Twenty-second Street.

A right on Twenty-second street? Wait a minute! Twenty-second was a one-way street. No problem except for one minor thing—they were going the wrong way!

"Use the wings!" Gretchen shouted. "Use the wings!"

"I'm trying!" the professor cried, hitting a button over and over again. "But she's still touching the car!"

BEEP . . . BEEP!

Somehow, they managed to squeeze between two family vans.

HOONNKKKK!

Then there was that garbage truck.

"AUGH! EEEK!"

And let's not forget all those pedestrians screaming and running for cover . . . including the telephone cable repair guys who leaped down their manhole to get out of the way.

Next, they took a left onto Lincoln Avenue. No problem . . . except Lincoln Avenue ended right on the small boat dock at Midvale Lake.

Putt . . . putt . . . sputter . . . sputter . . .

Sean looked at his sister. Her rocket skates had just run out of gas, and she was too tired to hang on to the car. Which was actually a good thing, because . . .

"Look out!" Gretchen shouted. "We're headed straight for the lake!"

"No problem!" the professor laughed. "Now that

she's no longer touching the paint, I'll just reach over and press this button here. . . ."

"AUGH . . ."
"WHOAA . . ."

Too late! The professor was just a little too overconfident and just a little too slow. They'd run out of dock and . . .

KA-SPLASH!!

. . . had found plenty of water, instead.

Fortunately, they were only a few yards from shore, and the car was in shallow water . . . where it sputtered to a stop and stuck fast to the floor of the muddy lake bottom.

A moment later, with lights flashing and siren blaring, the police car arrived on the scene. The chief and his partner emerged with their guns drawn, and they ordered the professor and his accomplice to get out of the car with their hands up.

The professor came out whining. "I haven't done anything wrong!" he shouted, staggering through the mud. Though he pretended to be crying, it was obvious to Sean that the man was really looking for some way to make a run for it. "It was all her fault!" He pointed at Gretchen, who was staggering beside him. "She's the one who wanted to drive the old woman crazy and get all her money. She made me do it!"

"Is that so!" Gretchen shouted angrily. She looked mad enough to punch him or hit him with something. But the only thing she had was the brown paper bag she'd been holding. So she gave it a swing and hit him over the head with it.

Ker-splat!

Of course it broke.

"EWWWWWW! What a mess!"

If the professor had any plans of trying to make an escape, he was now too grossed out to even move.

SATURDAY, 9:00 PDST

"Dad! We're going up to visit with Mrs. Sanks for a while," Melissa called. "She said Slobs could come up and chase a few rabbits if she wanted."

"That's great," Dad said, looking up from his breakfast. "And how is Mrs. Sanks these days?"

"She's fine," Sean answered. "Of course, she was really upset when she found out what Gretchen was up to."

"But," Melissa chimed in, "we're becoming pretty good friends with the sweet old lady."

"That's right," Sean said, grabbing an apple from the bowl on the table and munching away.

"She's kinda cool when you get to know her," Melissa explained.

Dad grinned and reached out to tousle her hair.

"Daaaad," Melissa complained.

"What?"

"She just spent the last couple hours brushing it," Sean explained.

Dad chuckled. "Listen, I hope you know how proud I am of both of you. And not just because you solved this case.

"I'm proud because there aren't too many kids your age who would be willing to spend a beautiful Saturday visiting with a lonely old woman."

"Sean's just in it for the tea and cookies," Melissa teased.

Dad smiled and continued. "And I know if your mom were here, she'd be proud of both of you, too."

"Well, since we're passing around compliments," Sean said, munching on his apple, "me and Misty, we're pretty proud of you, too."

"Of me? Why?"

"The way you told everybody there had to be a logical explanation for all that stuff happening. The way you stuck up for God and the Bible when you were on the radio."

Dad laughed. "God doesn't need anybody to stick up for Him. But if you stay on His side, you can't possibly go wrong."

"So we've noticed," Melissa laughed. "So we've noticed."

Meanwhile, across town at the Midvale Museum, a crate had just arrived, shipped all the way from Egypt.

"This is a great day for this museum," said the new curator as he watched workmen carry the crate into his building.

"But I've always heard there's a curse—" his assistant said.

"Curse shmurse!" snapped the curator. "That's only in the movies. This is Midvale. Nothing weird like that ever happens around here!"

Uh-oh. If he only knew. If he only knew. . . .

By Bill Myers

Children's Series:
Bloodhounds, Inc. — mystery/comedy
McGee and Me! — book and video
The Incredible Worlds of Wally McDoogle — comedy

Teen Series:
Forbidden Doors

Adult Novels:
Blood of Heaven
Threshold
Fire of Heaven

Nonfiction:
Christ B.C.
The Dark Side of the Supernatural
Hot Topics, Tough Questions
Faith Encounter

Picture Books:
Baseball for Breakfast